FIGHTING FOR KORA

BROTHERHOOD PROTECTORS WORLD

TEAM FALCO
BOOK FOUR

DEANNA L ROWLEY

Twisted Page Press LLC

Brotherhood Protectors Yellowstone World

Team Wolf

Guarding Harper - Desiree Holt

Guarding Hannah - Delilah Devlin

Guarding Eris - Reina Torres

Guarding Payton - Jen Talty

Guarding Leah - Regan Black

FIGHTING FOR KORA

TEAM FALCO BOOK 4

Deanna L. Rowley

CHAPTER 1

SETH FALCO GROANED as he reached out to slam his hand on the offending noise of his alarm, and scowled when he encountered nothing but air. He flopped his blankets back, and this time he growled when he couldn't find them. He quickly sat up, grabbed the alarm, threw it across the room, and sighed in relief when it shut off as it smashed against the far wall.

"What the hell?" Troy Falco demanded as he came into the room on a dead run. "What was that crash?"

"My alarm," Seth growled as he swung his legs to the side, and glared at his brother. "What are you doing in my room? Where's the coffee?"

Troy snickered at his oldest brother and laughed. "Perking in the kitchen, Esme is cooking the bacon, breakfast in a few. I have to ask, what time did you come in last night?"

"Two this morning. Nothing was happening at the mine, so Jake sent me home. At least I crashed here on the bed at two. What time is it now?"

"Six, shit, that means you're going to be a miserable prick at work for the next seventy-two hours, aren't you?"

"I'm a miserable prick all the time, why should the next seventy-two hours make any difference?" Seth scowled over his shoulder at his brother and withheld his grin as Troy shook his head at his comment.

"Take a shower, and I'll tell you at breakfast," Troy said as he backed out of Seth's bedroom. Before he closed the door, he looked back at Seth, and sighed, "Oh, by the way, we have guests for breakfast." Troy closed the door just as several pillows came flying toward him, yelling at Seth as to how much time he had before breakfast would be ready.

Seth groaned as he stood, scrubbed his face, and made a beeline to the attached bathroom. It had been a godsend to have Charli put a new bathroom in for him. He had found Paradise Ranch months ago and wanted to purchase it, so that he and all his siblings could live on it to become a family again. He knew he had been a bastard to them over the years, only meeting up with them when he had leave from the military, and never going home to see the old man after he left home at the age of seventeen. He loved his brothers, he really did, but my god, they could be intrusive at times. He hadn't realized how much he liked his privacy, until they all converged on his house every morning. He gave up trying to kick them out when he realized they liked his house, because he was the one with the best working kitchen. Not that he minded someone else cooking his breakfast for him. As a matter of fact, if one of his brothers or their girlfriends didn't cook breakfast, then he probably wouldn't eat. At almost forty years of age, he had yet to learn to cook. If he didn't have his brothers to invade his house in the morning, he'd have a strong cup of black coffee, maybe a couple slices of toast, and he would be fine. In no time he climbed into the lukewarm water and began his shower, finishing before it had become completely hot. In under ten minutes he was dressed, and not knowing the state of the house, since Charli was in the process of rebuilding her and Marcus' home, while helping with the renovations on the other homes, and everyone was staying with him until they were complete, it seemed like the situation at home changed daily, especially the placement of the furniture, or someone's clothes hanging off a chair, or the post leading up to the bedrooms, he grinned as he saw a shirt that looked like the one Trent had worn the day before hanging on the back of a chair. Shaking his head, hiding his smile, on a sigh he entered the kitchen, and gave a grunt when his brother Marcus handed him a cup of coffee before he was even three steps into the room. He might have grunted on the outside, but on the inside, he was grateful for the strong elixir. Seth made his way to the head of the table, and no one said a word until he had settled in his seat and drank at least half of the brew.

"What?" Seth scowled at the members of his family as he saw them staring at him.

"Several things," Troy was the first to speak, and seemed to be the one that always approached him. "First, how did it go at the mine?" Troy ignored the knock on the back door, and studied Seth as he talked, leaving one of the others to go open the door.

"A bust," Seth sighed in frustration as he refilled his cup and reached for the platter of bacon passed to him. "Jake finally sent me home when there was no activity. I won't be back for at least a week." He scowled then and looked at Troy. "I am on at the firehouse for the next seventy-two, right?" He paused with his handful of bacon hoovering over his plate as the newcomers walked in. "Patterson, Jake, what brings you here at the ass crack of dawn?" He pointed with his hand as he dropped half his handful of bacon back on the platter and passed it along to the others.

"We'll get to that in a minute," Hank said as he took the offered chair, and nodded to Chari who had brought them each a cup of coffee. "Continue, we can get to why we're here in a few." He nodded and sipped his coffee.

Troy continued his side of the conversation from before they were interrupted. "You are working the next seventy-two at the station, as well as the rest of us. I know it's unusual for us to all be there at the same time, but since the last fire, we're shorthanded until the injured get cleared to return to work. Not to mention that some are still out from that arson fire that covered up Chief Jade's murder a few months back."

"Speaking of clearing," Heath said as he joined them at the table. "Doesn't Garrison return to work today?"

"Yes, I got the call from the doctor two days ago that he cleared them to return to work."

"Which doctor?" Seth asked, and he didn't see his brothers exchange grins above his bent head, or the looks that passed between Hank, Jake, and Seth's brothers. They had talked while Seth was working for Jake at the Brotherhood Protection Agency that they were going to pair Seth with Garrison. Troy couldn't wait to see what his brother's reaction would be when he realized the returning firefighter was the woman who had spoken at their father's funeral months ago. Seth had made some pretty snide remarks about her, and Troy hadn't denied nor confirmed them, he couldn't wait to see what his brother's reaction would be.

"Both the physical and psych. Cleared by both of them."

"What happened?" Charli asked as she joined them at the table with a platter of scrambled eggs.

"Garrison was injured in the fire where the former Chief was murdered."

"The arson to cover it up?" Esme asked, joining them with the other platter of food. "I remember her from when I used to stop into the station to see Dad. It's not like we were close friends, but we knew each other enough to say hi to one another."

"I know her," Jake Cogburn spoke for the first time. "She's lived here for a few years, and we over at the Brotherhood know her. She's good people, and she comes into the Watering Hole sometimes. She's more friends with RJ than me, but since I'm married to RJ, then I know her more by association." The others nodded at his explanation, while they all noticed that Seth didn't really have an opinion of what they were discussing. Troy knew that would change in a heartbeat when Hank and Jake told him as to why they were there.

"Yes, Kora dislocated her shoulder in the blaze,

her doctor took her out of rotation and sent her to physical therapy. I know it's been a while, but she's good to go." Troy looked over at Seth with a smirk. "I'm assigning Garrison to you, Seth. I want you to keep an eye on her to see if she's really ready to return."

Seth looked up from his plate and gave his brother a dead stare, something he used to do with the recruits while he had been in the Marine Corps. For the life of him, he didn't understand why it didn't scare the ever-loving shit out of his siblings like it had the new recruits who had served under him. "Why would I have to keep an eye on her? You're the acting Chief, if you doubt her ability, then don't take her back. It's as easy as that."

"That's not the reason," Troy sighed, and looked at his siblings. When they nodded at him, he turned fully to his brother, and sighed heavily again. He pushed his plate away to fold his arms on the table in front of him. "There are several reasons why I'm pairing the two of you."

"Yeah? And what are they?" Seth didn't bother looking at his brother as he continued to eat. His brother's next words caused him to drop his fork and looked at him in horror, unable to form any words to convey his feelings. Everyone at the table was able to tell his thoughts by the expression on his face.

"Kora Garrison is the woman that spoke at

Dad's funeral. The one you commented on that was his lover. I know I never confirmed nor denied it, but she wasn't, and never was. However, they did have a history, that's why she was so upset at his funeral."

"What type of history?"

"It's not my story to tell, not because I don't want to tell it, but because I don't know all of it. All I know is that Dad acted as her mentor when she first became a firefighter." Troy shrugged. "I do know some other things, but like I just said, it's really not my business to tell you anything, other than I know for a fact that Kora and Dad were never an item intimately."

Seth didn't see his other siblings and their girlfriends studying him intently, and they sighed in relief when he shrugged and continued eating. "Whatever." He left it at that, and the others grinned at one another. Though they had a lot of issues they had already worked out since the men's father had passed away a few months ago, they still had a long way to go. Seth was the oldest of them all, and he had been the first one to leave home at the age of seventeen to join the Marines. He had never had a very good relationship with his father after his mother had perished in a fire, and the older he'd gotten, the more he'd looked like his mother, which caused his father to resent him. Seth had saved his twin brothers from the fire, Marcus was born years later from their father's second marriage, and he didn't find out about Heath until later. It turned out that Heath came from an affair their father had while still married to Carmen, Seth's mother.

Seth had kept in contact with all his brother via e-mail and phone calls, but since the second he left home to join the military, he never, not once, came home. The next time he saw his father, was twenty-years later at his funeral, which happened to be this past spring. At the funeral, a friend of theirs, Hank Patterson, who owned the Brotherhood Protection Agency, the man currently sitting at his table, oper-ated his agency in several locations, contacted the brothers and asked them to come to Colorado, Fool's Gold to be precise, and become firefighters for the Fool's Gold station. When the former Chief had died, it had been ruled a homicide, and then the killer had set a fire to cover up the murder. Didn't work as well as he had planned, because the investigation worked, and they caught the guy. Troy was the lead investigator on that case, and had to protect Esme, the former chief's daughter from the arsonist/murderer.

At Shawn Falco's funeral, Seth, who hadn't been home for twenty years, and only saw him for all of ten minutes before he passed was shocked at how many people had shown up. What had doubly shocked him was all the people who had such nice things to say about the man he considered was a worthless human being, and a bad parent to boot. Maybe he had gotten that impression from Shawn being a worthless parent, but all he could remember was the beautiful woman who has spoken at his father's funeral, and she had nothing but great, glowing compliments to say about the man. Seth's first impression had been that the two of them were lovers, and no one had told him differently.

What really pissed Seth off was the fact that he couldn't get the woman out of his mind. It seemed like whenever he let his guard down, she was right there in his thoughts. Her long red hair, piercing blue eyes, and to die for figure. A figure that he wanted to get his hands all over, and hadn't been able to stop thinking about since his father's funeral. He had thought he was a pervert, because he had been lusting after his father's mistress, but now, if he could believe his brother, they never had been lovers.

"Okay," Seth said as he looked at his brother, pushed his plate away, and picked up his cooling cup of coffee. As he sipped, he looked over at the two men sitting at his table. *I guess, technically, you could call them his boss.*

"What brings you two here?"

Hank drew in a deep breath, then let it out

slowly. "It's about Garrison." His statement left a dead silence in its wake.

"What about her?" All five of the Falco brothers asked as one.

"You know that we're still looking into the fire, even though we've caught the guy that killed Chief Jade, correct?" Jake Cogburn said as he looked around the table. "In the course of the Brotherhood's investigation, we've uncovered someone that is out to get Garrison. We have no idea why, or how, or when. All we have to go on mostly is a hunch, and our guts, hell, we don't even have anything solid. All we have is an overheard conversation in a bar, and the tip came in from a person under the influence."

"And?" Seth sat forward, and demanded, "What are you saying?"

"We're saying," Hank sighed as he settled back into his chair. "That you, Seth, need to one, keep an eye on Kora Garrison, two, protect her at all costs."

"Why me?" Seth scowled at them, and wasn't worried that he would be reprimanded for talking to them that way.

"Because, you are a Captain with the fire department, Garrison is a Lieutenant. It is my understanding that she would work directly under you and take directions from you."

Seth's mind immediately flashed to the woman who has spoken at his father's funeral, but this time she was naked and beneath him. It took several seconds to get his thoughts back on the conversation.

"Does she know she's in any trouble?"

"No, and I'd like to keep it that way, because we have no clue if the information, we received is correct, or if it was just a drunk calling in a prank. We would like to err on the side of caution here."

Seth looked around the table at his siblings and their girlfriends, and saw different degrees of concern, shock, and he wouldn't say fear, but he remembered when each of them had been in a position where one of his brothers had to protect them. On a heavy sigh, he looked at the two men and asked one question, "Is she to know I'm protecting her?"

"No, and, Seth," Jake leaned forward and grinned. "Be careful. Kora Garrison can give as good as she gets, and she's sharp as a tack. It'll take a strong person to protect her. She's lived here in Fool's Gold for several years now, and like Troy, I don't know her story, and I didn't pry into her past, but from what I've seen and heard over the years, she has no one to rely on. No family that is, but she does have friends, and my RJ is one of them. Don't make me go home and tell RJ that we let something bad happen to Kora. She went apeshit on me when she found out Kora had been injured during that arson fire."

"Fine, I'll do it, but I'm telling you now that we're going to have to find a way to tell her. I'm not going to go around following her to try to protect her without her knowledge. One, I don't work that way, two, we have no idea who each other is, and I'm not going to have her call Faulkner to come arrest my ass for harassment, or for being her stalker.

Seth didn't say a word as his siblings snickered, he only threw them a glare, and shook his head when they only grinned back at him.

"Wow," Marcus said from his spot at the table. "This is the woman that spoke at Dad's funeral?"

"Yes, the one that stood there and told everyone what a wonderful man the asshole was," Seth said as he finished his coffee, and quickly stood. "I'll meet you guys at the station." He left them staring after him, and no one said a word until they heard the back door shut behind him. Once they heard a vehicle start, they all turned to Troy.

"What's that about?" Heath scowled at him.

Troy grinned at them before he shrugged and looked at Esme. "After the funeral, when Seth mentioned something about Kora being Dad's lover, I never denied nor confirmed his suspicions." He shrugged again, then grinned at the others. "I may even had said that she would have been Dad's type."

"Isn't she the one Dad saved from an apartment

fire when she was like eleven or twelve? Then when she got older, she became a firefighter, because Dad was her hero?" Trent, Troy's twin asked in confusion. "Holy shit, you let Seth think Kora was Dad's lover?"

"That will go over like a ton of bricks," Heath chuckled, suddenly anxious to get to the firehouse to see what type of fireworks there would be for the next three days. They exchanged grins with Hank and Jake as they stood to leave, wishing them luck with their observations of what was about to happen. Each of the men had their own thoughts and theories on how Seth would handle the situation. None of them really knew their oldest brother, and that was one of the reasons they all stayed at Paradise Ranch. One, because it was Seth's, though he continuously told them that it belonged to all of them, and when Hank Patterson and Jake Cogburn asked them to come to Fool's Gold to work as firefighters, they had no place to stay, and Seth had said he had bought the place because he had wanted to get to know his brothers again. The twins and Marcus had been young when he'd left for the service, and Heath had been sixteen when he confronted Shawn that he was the old man's son. Seth had heard all about it through letters, and phone calls with the twins, and because their father was dead and gone now, Seth felt that it was time to get to know his brothers, and had offered them a place to stay while they established themselves in the Fool's Gold firehouse.

It had been boring lately, except for the wildfire they'd fought last month, now it was time to see what type of fireworks they could see at the station with Kora returning to work after being gone most of the summer with a dislocated shoulder injury from a previous fire.

The others quickly cleaned up the table, and while the men got ready to head to the station, where they would be living for the next seventy-two hours, the women got on with their own morning routines.

CHAPTER 2

Kora Garrison tossed her blankets back, reached out to shut off the alarm before it even rang, and was in the shower in minutes. She had trouble sleeping the night before because of her excitement at returning to work after being out for months. With both her doctor and physical therapists approval in her hand, she had gone to the department shrink and had a long talk with her about her returning. It took a couple of days to hear back from her, but Dr. Nanci signed off on Kora going back to her job, stating she had the mental clarity to resume her duties, and the injury she'd sustained in the fire that took the life of her former chief, hadn't affected her mental ability to continue working.

Kora had immediately called Troy Falco, the acting chief at the firehouse where she worked and told him that she had been cleared by everyone to return to duty. He told her to report at seven Friday morning, and she would be on for seventy-two hours. That was three days ago, and today was the day she was to report in. Her returning would be two-fold. One, she would be sad that her old chief would not be there, since he had been murdered, and the murderer had started a fire to cover up the crime, which was where Kora and several other firefighters had been injured. Kora herself had dislocated her shoulder when a beam had fallen on her as she'd fought the fire, causing her to miss work for the last few months.

The second issue Kora had was that she didn't know any of the new firefighters that had been hired to either fill in or replace the firefighters that had been injured in the same fire as her. She knew Troy, she had known him, because his father had saved her from a burning building when she was eleven years old. Because of Shawn Falco, she had gone on to become a firefighter herself, and had worked in his station back in Denver. When the opportunity to work in Fool's Gold had come up, Shawn had encouraged her to take the position. He had even written a glowing letter of recommendation when she'd applied to become a Lieutenant with the fire department, and because of her scores, she had passed and been promoted. She had been in Fool's Gold for years before she learned that her old friend and mentor had passed away. Because she had been out on medical leave due to her injury during the arson fire that took Chief Jade from them, Kora had gone to the funeral to pay her respects. She hadn't been surprised by all the other fellow firefighters in attendance that had shown their respect to the wonderful man he had been. The thing that had really shocked her was the fact that Shawn had five sons in attendance, she knew about Troy, and knew he had brothers, but had never seen them before, not even when she'd started as a firefighter and worked in Shawn's firehouse. Kora remembered that Shawn would only admit that he had children, not once in all the years she'd known him had he ever talked about them, let alone bragged about them. It had been a shock to learn they had all served in one branch of the military or another.

After her shower, Kora dressed in her uniform of dark-blue cargo pants, and a dark-blue tee shirt that had Fool's Gold Fire written in yellow across her back, with the fire department logo over her left breast, embroidered over her right breast were her name and rank. She made sure the bag she'd packed the night before had everything she needed, and satisfied, she went into her kitchen and started a pot of coffee. Because she had known she'd be gone for seventy-two hours, she hadn't stocked up on groceries for a few days. She cooked up the last of the eggs, and toasted the last two slice of bread for her breakfast. She would swing by and pick up more food on her way home in three days when she finished her shift.

After breakfast, she cleaned the area, and because the date on the milk was the day before, she took it with her on her way to her truck and with the small baggie of cat food she'd brought with her, she fed the cats that she knew lived in the alley. There had been several times she'd tried to catch them and bring them into her home, but no matter what she did, they avoided capture at all costs. Instead, she fed them every day. She didn't know if they caught mice, or whatever, but it made her feel better that she made sure they had something to eat. She quickly cleaned out a bowl, dumped the food in it, then took the other bowl and poured the little bit of milk left in the jug into the second bowl, tossing the now empty jug into the nearby dumpster. From experience Kora knew if she stayed to wait for the cats to appear, she'd be waiting all day, so she stepped back and headed to her truck.

It took a few minutes to get settled into her truck, and with a grin on her face, she looked over at the food dishes she'd just filled and saw the six cats eating from both bowls. Happy, she quickly pulled out of her parking spot and headed to the fire station that she hadn't set foot in for over two months. She used to stop in all the time after the fire, but Troy had taken her aside and asked her to stay away until she was completely healed. He had explained that he didn't want her to set her physical and/or mental healing back with being in the firehouse every day. Though she didn't like it, Kora had done as he wished, and this would be her first day back in several weeks. She wondered how everyone was doing, and couldn't wait to catch up with the others.

Thirty minutes later she pulled into the fire station and grinned when she found 'her' parking spot empty, where she immediately parked, shut the vehicle off, grabbed her go bag, and exited her truck. She knew she was early, but Kora wanted to get a chance to talk with the outgoing firemen and women before they left for their three days off. It had been weeks since she'd seen anyone.

It didn't take long before the people in the firehouse to notice her, since she walked directly through the bays that housed the trucks, then into the back where they hung out while on duty. Kora went directly to the room she would be sleeping in, and placed her bag on the made-up bed, and grinned when the woman who came out of the showers gave a start when she saw her.

"Kora! Are you back?" Desiree cried out as she rushed forward and hugged Kora. Once she stepped back, the two of them laughed as Desiree quickly dressed, and began tossing her things into her own bag. In minutes she was packed, and Kora was unpacked. Together they walked down to the kitchen, and everyone jumped to their feet when Kora entered, and before she could get to the coffee pot, every man, at least twelve of them, hugged her and asked how she was doing. When she finally made it to the coffee pot, she had turned down all of their offers for breakfast, stating she'd eaten before she left her home. She settled down and watched as they filled their plates, and waited until they settled around the table. From past experience, she knew the kitchen would be spotless before the next shift arrived in two hours. She hadn't realized how early she was in her excitement to get to the firehouse.

"How has everyone been?" Kora asked as they all settled down to eat.

They all said they were good, then they asked how she was, and she quickly explained that she had been cleared to return to work by her PCP, the Physical Therapist, and the psych doctor.

"What about your 1582?" Desiree asked as she shoveled a forkful of scrambled eggs into her mouth and washed it down with a drink of orange juice.

"A what?" Kora scowled at her.

"You know, the 1582," one of the other firefighters said. "In a nutshell it's the department's physical fitness test you have to perform before returning to work, regardless of what your regular doctor says. This test is from the fire department, no getting out of it. It's basically the same test we all take annually. Matter of fact, most of us have to take it when the next shift comes in."

"Oh, where would I get one of those done?"

"Three can give you one," another firefighter laughed as he said that, and the others joined in, causing Kora to frown at them. "He's giving them out today at the training facility next door."

"Why do I feel like I'm missing something?"

"You've been gone since the fire that took Chief Jade from us, and a lot of things have changed around here. Personally, from my perspective, it's all for the better," Tom nodded as he sipped his coffee. "Literally when the ashes settled from the fire that turned out to be an arson to cover up Chief Jade's murder, and where you and the others were injured, all hell broke loose. Troy Falco came in as acting chief, he was a fire investigator for his old house over in Denver, and he brought his four brothers with him."

"Falco?" Kora sat up straighter, and looked at her coworkers in shock. "Any relation to Shawn Falco?"

"No clue who that is," Tom shrugged. "But Troy and his brothers all have the same last name, and you know how we use them during a fire, well, it was the oldest one that started using the numbers."

"How? What numbers?"

"One is for the oldest, two is the second oldest, and down the line. We really only use the numbers during a fire, it's easier to keep them apart."

"Please, explain it to me."

"Okay, you're in the middle of a fire and you call out, 'Falco, I need the hose on the northwest wall." Desiree began.

"I understand that, it's been done before."

"Correct, but if you call out Falco, there are five of them."

"Ah, now I understand, and if you said Troy is the acting Chief and he is number three, then he would be outside monitoring the situation and directing everyone."

"Exactly, it works well when we've done it in the past."

"Are the others specialized in anything in particular?"

"Seth, number one, has twenty years' experience as a Marine. Well, all of them are former military, but One has the most experience. He is the oldest of them all. I believe his specialty is gas and chemical. Two specializes in Wildland firefighting, I forget his name. He's not always here in the house, but comes in to work out with his brothers, and goes on calls if he's needed. Three is Troy, and he's our acting Chief, he's also a twin. Four is three's twin, his name is Trent, and he is a fire investigator."

"And five?" Kora asked when everyone stopped talking.

"Five's name is Marcus. He specializes in gas and chemical fires, the same as One, and operates a helicopter. It comes in handy during our fires if we need one."

Kora sat there and absorbed that information. She listened to the others talk as they finished their meal, and continued to sit there as they cleaned up after themselves. By the time the kitchen was spotless, and a fresh pot of coffee was brewing, she looked up when she heard a door slam, and the most handsome man she had ever laid her eyes on, who also wore a very pissed-off expression, stormed into the kitchen, tossed his go bag on a chair, and demanded, "Who the hell parked in *my* parking spot."

When no one said a word, Kora scowled when everyone looked at her and she shrugged, then laughed at the guy. "Was your name on it?"

"No, but I've been parking in the third spot from the back door since I started working here."

"That's *my* spot," Kora said, and turned to look at him. "I've been parking there for the last four *years*. If you would have paid attention, then you would have seen that the sign attached to the building has *my* name on it."

"Not since I've been here, you haven't, and there's no name on that space."

"Yeah, well, I've been out on medical leave, so now that I'm back, we'll see whose spot it is. Maybe you should get your eyes checked, or pay attention and look at the sign."

"Please, move your truck."

"No." By this time Kora had stood and placed her fisted hands on her hips, and glared at him. He mimicked her stance, and glared right back.

Before she could say anything, he demanded of her, "Who are you, and what are you doing here? Only authorized personnel are allowed in the firehouse."

Kora noticed no one came to her defense, but she didn't back down.

"Who are you?" she demanded, instead of answering him.

"I'm Falco," Seth said, and before Kora could say anything, she heard someone from behind her say, "One."

The two of them continued to glare at one another for several minutes, and it wasn't until someone else spoke that they broke apart.

"Garrison!" Came a cry from the entrance to the kitchen and Kora tore her gaze from the man before her and broke out in a gigantic grin.

"Troy!" She hurried over to him and gave him a side hug. "How are you? I had heard you were the acting Chief. How is everything working out for you?"

"Good, good, we'll get to all that, but first, what's going on between you and Seth? I walked in here and could cut the tension with a knife."

"*She's* parked her truck in *my* spot," Seth growled from directly behind Kora, and the sound of his voice, along with his manly scent sent a delicious tingle down her back. She didn't think anyone saw her reaction to his close proximity until she saw Desiree's smirk. Kora only grinned at her friend, then focused on what the two brothers were saying.

"Fight nicely children," Troy said. "I'm not going to get between you on who parks where. As long as my parking space is free and clear, I don't care, figure it out yourselves." He nodded to the two of them and when Kora nodded back, he winked at her before turning to his brother. "We good?"

"Fine, but it's my spot."

"Stow it, Seth," Troy said. "I'm going to say this one time in front of everyone, so they know where I'm coming from. You may be the oldest of us Falco brothers, and I respect you in that way, I also defer to your better judgement, but when it comes to this firehouse, *I* am the one in charge, and someone parking in your alleged space isn't an issue, don't make it one, or I will assign spaces to everyone.

"No!" Several people said as one, and they all glared at Seth.

"Fine," Seth sighed as he bent to pick up his bag, then turned to glare at Kora. "What time do you get here?"

"Whenever I pull into the parking lot," she snarked back, not giving him the answer he wanted with an actual time. She held in her snicker at his glare until he stormed away from them. Troy only shook his head and walked over to the coffee pot.

"I only have one thing to say."

"Which is?"

"Don't come to me when he harasses you about your parking spot."

"Or when he snarks about anything else," came a voice from the side, and Kora turned to study the man who held out his hand to her. "Trent Falco, or number four." They shook, and she was quickly introduced to the others as they got their coffee.

"The only way I'd come to you was if he mistreated me, or won't help in a fire."

"Understood." Troy nodded as he filled his coffee cup, took a sip, then looked at her. "You have your clearance paperwork?"

"I do."

"Bring it to my office, then we can discuss your 1582."

"I'll be doing that," came a voice from the door-way, and they all looked at Seth as he stood there. It took everything Kora had not to drool at the sight of him. "Remember, we were going to have that house-wide challenge today for the leaving shift, and on-coming shift? It's been almost a year since most of the men and women here have been given their physicals. Thought this would be a perfect time."

Troy looked at Seth with a scowl, then saw several people enter, and they were not only the people he worked with on the incoming shift, but also people who had been on yesterday's day shift, and should have had the weekend off. Luckily, he knew the challenge would be only for a couple of hours, three or four at the most, so he felt better about everyone being recertified. Before he could say anything, he didn't know whether it shocked him or not when Seth nodded, and said, "Paper-work is already on your desk."

"Thanks," Troy sighed heavily and with his cup in his hand, he looked at everyone as they began to arrive. "Garrison, my office with your paperwork, everyone else, get with Seth to start this year's challenge."

Kora waited until Troy turned to leave, and as she followed him, the man named Seth stepped in front of her to stop her.

"Fifteen minutes, then I want you in the back lot for the challenge."

"I'll be there." She winked at him, then blew him a kiss. She knew it was unprofessional, and she had never acted like that around a man before. It was unprofessional, but there was something about the way this man carried himself that Kora wanted to throw him for a loop to see how he would react. No one said a word when he actually growled, and it was Troy who shook his head at her as they walked down the hallway to his office.

CHAPTER 3

"WHAT THE HELL?" Seth growled under his breath as the redheaded woman winked at him as she followed Troy down the hall. He looked around at the others, and knew immediately they would be no help, because they stood there grinning at him.

"Outside," he barked out as he turned on his heel and strode toward the empty lot behind their firehouse. Seth ignored the comments from the newcomers as to who had pissed in his Wheaties as he strode toward the lot on the other side of the firehouse. Luckily, he had called ahead to one of the outgoing firemen and had him set up the equipment they would need. He was glad he had, because it saved a lot of time, and he knew the outgoing firemen wanted to leave as soon as they were done with their physicals.

Seth turned and faced the people as they continued to stream out of the back of the building and into the lot. He waited until they were all there, then nodded as Troy and the woman who had taken his parking spot joined them.

"I called you all here today because several of us need to have our yearly re-certification physicals. It has also been brought to my attention that Garrison needs to have her 1582, aka fitness physical, before she can return to work. After talking it over with the powers that be, we decided we would all do it today."

"What about you?" Someone in the crowd called out, and Seth looked around to find out who had asked. Not seeing anyone, he nodded once, then stood before them with a tall and straight posture.

"Myself included. This is why Troy will be here to help. As you all know, I am unable to judge myself, and Troy, being the Chief can't pass himself. We are here to make sure we both pass."

"Won't the fact that you are brothers make you slack off on the other?" Kora called out, and stood there just as tall and proud as Seth did. They glared at one another for several minutes until someone stepped forward to stand beside Seth.

"That's where we come in," the new man said. "I'm Heath Falco, and though I've fought fires with these men, I'm here to make sure it's all above board. I am a Wildland firefighter and though I work out of this house, I too need my re-certification."

"Thank you for telling me that, but you're also their brother, what's to say that you won't turn your head when they don't do as well as they should? Or when they miss a step coming back from the fifth floor in the tower?" Kora asked again. This time she crossed her arms over her chest and cocked a hip out to one side as she studied the men standing at the front of the group, staring back at them.

"Because, I'll be keeping an eye on them," Tom stepped forward and joined the men at the front of the crowd. "Is that okay for you?"

"It is, thank you. I trust you, and no offense to the others, I don't know them enough to trust them. At least not yet." Kora nodded, then uncrossed her arms.

The entire time Kora talked, Seth couldn't take his eyes off her. He couldn't wait to see what she was about, and whether she could handle what he had planned for the crew. What he hoped no one knew was that his interaction with her over the parking spot caused him to get hard at her feistiness, something he never thought he liked in a woman. He didn't know if it was Kora herself, or the interaction between them, but he was turned on every time he looked at her. He really liked the fact that she didn't back down from him, or his brothers. It seemed like she could give as well as she got in any situation, and he couldn't wait to put it to a test. The only downside of his liking of her, and calmed his blood was the fact that he knew she had been his father's former lover, and since he had hated his old man since a young age, he knew he would never get together sexually with someone who had been with the man he had hated most of his life.

On a heavy sigh, he looked out at the others standing before him, and nodded when he saw his brother Troy in the back of the crowd holding up a stopwatch, along with Tom, who stood beside him.

"Okay then, let's get this show started!" Seth called out as he clapped his hands a couple of times and brought up the rear.

"Who's going first?" Kora called out as they gathered to the side of the training area in the back of their firehouse.

"I think," Tom said as he stepped forward, and didn't continue until he had everyone's attention. "I think, Kora, you need to go first. You've been out on medical leave for the last few months, and since you can't even clock in until you pass your fitness physical, you should go first."

"Got it," Kora said as she held up her finger, and

disappeared into the back of the fire station. When she came back outside, Seth stared at her in shock.

"You don't have to wear your boots!" he called out to her as he stormed forward.

"Hey, you do your recertification your way, I'll do mine, my way."

"Whatever, probie."

"What did you call me?" Kora demanded as she reached out and grabbed his arm and whipped him back around to face her.

"Probie."

"*My* name is *Lieutenant* Garrison, and if anyone is the probie around here, it's you. I have been with this house for several years, hence it's *my* parking spot. You're the newbie around here, you've been here what? Three, maybe four months?"

"*I* am *Captain* Falco. You weren't here when I came here." Seth glared at her, and he noted that they both had the same stance with their hands fisted on their hips as they bored holes into each other.

"It wasn't my fault that a beam fell on me while I was fighting a fire that was deliberately set to cover up the fact that the asshole arsonist killed my Chief. I was doing my job, and took one for the team. You weren't here, so don't tell me how to do my job!" She glared at him, and she would never know why he suddenly held up his hands and backed away from her.

"Sorry," he mumbled, then waved his hand at her in a grand gesture. "Whatever, you do you. Don't come crying on my shoulder when you fail. Just remember, we must work closely together if we're going to get this firehouse back to where it was before the former Chief was murdered."

"Ha! Eat my dust!" She looked over at Troy and Tom and nodded. "I'm ready." She waited until the two men came up to her and as soon as she received the go ahead, Kora immediately donned her coat, vest, air tank, helmet, and the gloves she had always worn while fighting a fire. She only paused long enough to take a deep breath, let it out slowly, then she nodded once as Tom told her to go. She immediately cleared her mind, and ignored everyone around her as she walked up to the table with the hose bundle and rolled it off onto her shoulder. With the single focus of being the best of the best and beating her own personal time from doing this same fitness test in the past, Kora walked to the drill tower and disappeared inside, with both Tom and Troy hot on her heels watching to make sure she didn't miss any steps on the way back down.

"What the hell?" Seth mumbled to himself when he heard several people suck in their breath and he looked up and saw Kora emerge from the tower. He stayed off to the side, trying to remember what time she'd begun while he watched her go through the next four steps of the physical. He didn't know whether it frustrated him or not when she completed the entire course, and no one called out her time.

Seth watched as the others he worked with went through their physical, and when it was his time, he kept on his combat boots, and cargo pants. In his head he figured he would beat Garrison's time, because he didn't wear the heavy boots and pants of the turn-out gear they wore during the fire. Because this was only a recertification physical, he only had to wear the required equipment of the coat, vest, air tank, helmet, and gloves. His lower body was what he wore every day. By the time he drove the 150-pound I-beam the five feet across the mark, he was wiping the sweat from his brow. He looked up with a grin when everyone cheered him on, and felt a jolt in both the region of his heart and his cock when the first person he saw was Kora, and she not only winked at him, but she also blew him what he considered a raspberry, especially when she did it all with a wrinkled nose.

Kora stood off to the side after her turn and watched the others. She was particularly interested in how the man named Seth would do. As she watched him, she was impressed by not only his speed, but his precision, if she had to guess, she would say he had some military experience in his past. The only thing worrying her now was that if he really was the new Captain, then she would have to work under him. At the sudden image of her being beneath him with them both naked, she had to step away to get a bottle of water to cool herself down as the images flashed across her brain. It took several minutes for them to disappear before she could concentrate on the tests around her. She felt confident she had passed, and hoped she'd beat her time from last year. In order for her to return to work, she had to have done her fitness physical in less than seven minutes. Anything over that time and she would have failed, and wouldn't be able to return to work until she passed it. She was confident that she'd done her best time. While her dislocated shoulder had healed, she'd been working with her physical therapist in exercises to work her upper body, and when she received the go ahead to resume her regular exercises from her regular doctor, she had started going to the gym. Not only had she worked and built up her upper-body strength, she'd lost at least twenty-five pounds. As a personal challenge to herself she had donned her fire boots, as well as her fire pants, knowing they added extra weight to her. It was a personal challenge to pass the test with the extra weight. If something happened and she failed the test, she wouldn't wear them in the next test.

"Damn girl," Desiree said to Kora as she came over with a bottle of water and wiped the sweat off her brow. She had just completed her own test. "I was nowhere near as fast as you. I only hope I clocked in under the seven-minute mark."

"Me too," Kora sighed, and they drank their water and watched the others complete their test. It took almost two hours to get everyone done, and Kora liked that Desiree was asked to help Tom time the Falco brothers, while they in turn clocked Tom.

"What now?" Kora asked when everyone had gone through the course, and they began taking care of the hoses and equipment used. By this time, she had removed her fire boots and pants, and placed them back at her locker in the station, changing back into her regular work boots she wore while not in her fire gear.

"We wait for the other captains to tally up the scores," Seth said as he came up behind them, and picked up the almost sixty-pound hose bundle from the first exercise and carried it to where it belonged. As the rest of the firefighters cleaned up the area and put the equipment away, Kora helped, and didn't know if it was in frustration or joy when the alarm went off before they were told what their scores were. She did know that if anyone failed, then they couldn't go out on a call until they passed the physical.

When no one stopped her from rushing back

into the firehouse to get her gear to answer the call, she grinned as she donned her gear again, then looked up at Eric, another fireman, and asked, "What do you have?" When Eric kept looking behind her, she swung around, then swore as she saw Seth standing there. "Sorry."

"What do you have?" Seth asked as they finished donning their gear, and rushed to the fire engine. While Seth climbed into the passenger seat, Eric crawled behind the wheel, and Kora took her regular position behind Eric, allowing her to get any instructions from Seth on the way to the fire.

"Small brush fire out of town," Eric said, and Kora noticed someone had hopped into the front seat of the Wildland Fire truck and followed them out of town.

"I wasn't here last month, but how bad was the one then?" she asked and looked at Seth as he turned to look at her.

"Bad, but we were able to contain it quickly. Heath almost lost his life in it, but with his experience in fighting wildfires he and Tessa were able to survive. He did hurt his knee, but he's still able to work the ladder truck if needed."

Kora wanted to ask him who those people were, but figured the front of the cab of a fire engine on the way to a fire wasn't the time or place. She watched the scenery as they blew through town to head to the scene of the fire. As soon as they arrived, they all jumped from their trucks, grabbed their equipment, and got to work.

~

Kora stood there with her hands on her hips, drinking a bottle of water, and staring off at the burnt remains of the fire they had finished extinguishing. It had taken hours, but they were able to stop it before it spread any more. She looked up as Seth and the man she'd learned was referred to as Two during a fire, otherwise known as Heath approached her.

"We're ready to pack it in," Seth said as he drank his own bottle of water, and poured the rest over his head.

"Okay." Kora nodded at him, then turned to head back to the truck, so they could head back to the station. She saw another fireman approach them, and the next thing she knew, she was pushed to the ground, and someone was on top of her. She didn't know when she'd lost her helmet. Before she could say anything, Seth leaned down and ground out.

"Do. Not. Move." Kora could only nod, but she listened to the orders being given above her. It was confusing, but she knew eventually she would understand, but for right now, she would do as told. Later she would determine it had been the tone of Seth's voice that had her sitting still for so long. After what seemed like hours, but was only about ten minutes, she was helped to her feet, handed her helmet, and escorted back to the fire truck and hustled in to her regular seat. As the door began to shut, she heard Troy tell Seth that he would call it in, and they quickly left to head back to the station.

Kora sighed in relief when Eric backed the fire engine into the station, shut it off, and she climbed out of the truck. It had been months since she'd fought her last fire, and though she'd kept up with her exercises, she hadn't realized how heavy those hoses were. She didn't know if she was exhausted because of the fire, she'd just fought, or because of what happened afterward. She was still in the dark about everything that had occurred, especially from her position beneath Seth, but she'd get to the bottom of it now that they were back. As soon as she removed her turn-out gear and slipped her feet into her regular boots, she made a beeline to the kitchen, and sighed in relief when the coffee pot had just stopped perking.

She looked up as the others joined her, and stepped to the side as they reached for their own coffee cups. She scowled when she saw there were five cups with only numbers on them. "What's up with that?" She pointed with her cup to those, and they frowned, then grinned at her.

"I'm number One because I'm the oldest of us five," Seth said as he pulled out a chair at the table, and Kora noted it was beside the one she always sat in. She couldn't resist making a comment.

"I see you didn't take *my* place at the table."

"I was told not to sit there," he said, and left it at that. As they settled in to drink their coffee, he sighed heavily. "We need to write up our reports for that fire. Troy's waiting for someone to arrive, then we have to go in and talk with him."

"I just want a cup of coffee first before I start it."

"I understand." Seth nodded as he sipped from his own cup, and looked up when his brother Troy, the chief of the fire station joined them. "What's up?"

"First, they're on their way, second, we didn't get to do this before the call came in, but I have the results of the fitness tests."

Kora sat up quickly, crossed her hands on the table before her, then grinned at Troy. "I passed, right? Because neither you nor Tom held me back from responding to the fire, I passed?"

"You did." Troy nodded, then looked around as the other members of the station came closer. "As a matter of fact, you were the only one to get a hundred."

"What?" Seth demanded as he jerked his head between the two of them. "What was her time?"

"Six minutes even."

"Yes!" Kora yelled as she put her fist in the air, and did a happy dance in her seat.

"What was *my* score?" Seth demanded as he glared at his brother.

Troy grinned as he studied his brother and with a big production, he said, "You came in with a score of ninety-five. You missed scoring a hundred by only half a second, with six minutes, thirty point four nine seconds."

"Son of a bitch." Seth scowled, then turned his glare on Kora. "I want a rematch."

"Next year," she laughed as she stood and headed to refill her cup. "And to think, I wore my complete turn-out gear and still got the highest score. I'll be in the office writing up my report if you need me." She laughed all the way down the hall, doing a happy dance a couple of times in her excitement.

Seth watched her and sighed before he turned back to his brother. "You were joking about the numbers, right? To make her feel good after being out of work for so long? I got a hundred also, right?"

"Sorry, but no, you got what I told you. That was from both Tom and my stopwatches."

"Shit," Seth said, then looked at his cup of coffee for several minutes before he looked up and grinned. "Guess I'd better hit the gym more."

"Shit," Troy sighed, and knew that Seth would

drag all his brothers out to run with him and use his equipment in his basement when they weren't on duty. He was glad Esme was okay with his working out, and wouldn't be upset when he had to leave their bed early on his days off.

CHAPTER 4

KORA LEANED back in her chair and stretched the stiff muscles in her neck from being bent over the desk for so long. It had been so long since she'd been at the fire station that it was taking her a while to get the kinks out, then back into the rhythm of things. If she had only sustained a dislocated shoulder from her injury she would have been back to work sooner, but since she'd also tore a ligament, that the doctors hadn't found right away, she had been out of work for almost four months. From what she'd seen earlier, a lot of things had changed while she'd been out. The jury was still out on whether they were good or bad changes. At the knock on her door, she looked up and grinned at the two men standing there.

"Come in," Kora said as she quickly stood, and held out her hand to Hank Patterson and Jake

Cogburn. Once she welcomed them, and they settled in the chairs before her desk, she asked, "What brings you here?"

"Heard you started back to work today, and I was in town discussing some things with Jake. I wanted to come and welcome you back. I'll be out of town for a couple of weeks and won't have the opportunity to do it later." Before Kora could respond, she scowled at the five men as they began filing into her small office, and it was Seth who shut the door behind them, then made his way over to stand behind her as the others leaned against the other furniture in the room, leaving Hank and Jake to sit in the chairs before her desk.

"What's going on?" Kora scowled at everyone, then because she knew his wife, and him, she turned to look onto Jake. "Cog? What's going on?"

Jake didn't waste any time in telling her, but he led his explanation with a question. "Who did you piss off?"

Taking the question literally, Kora leaned back in her chair with a smirk. "Him," she said as she threw her thumb in Seth's direction. Her response caused the brothers to snort a laugh, or chuckle.

"Okay, let me rephrase that," Jake said. "Who did you piss off enough to want you dead?"

"Excuse me?" Kora sat up quickly, and would have jumped to her feet it Seth hadn't laid his hand gently on her shoulder to stop her. The feel of his warm hand sent shivers down her spine, and she remained seated. "What's going on?" She felt like she was repeating herself, but no one seemed to be answering her questions. She turned her head enough to glare at Seth, and he sat on the edge of her desk, looking down at her, ignoring the rest of the men in the room.

"Do you know what Hank and Jake do for a living?"

"Yes, Hank owns an agency called the Brother-hood Protectors. He started one over in Montana, then he opened a branch of that agency here in Fool's Gold. Jake is in charge of it. Before you ask, I know Jake and his wife, RJ, along with Gunny. In case you don't know them, he is RJ's father. I go to their bar all the time."

"Okay, since you know what Jake and Hank are all about, this should be easier to explain than I thought."

"Explain how?"

"Hank hired us Falco brothers to come work for the Fool's Gold fire department just after Chief Jade was murdered. I'm surprised you didn't see them at our father's funeral. Anyway, Hank asked us to come here because of the murder, and arson. We all have experience being firefighters from our time in the military. I was a Marine Corps Fire-fighter, what they called a MOS7051, and I worked expeditionary firefighting and rescue. I'm trained in all aspects of firefighting, but I specialized in Aircraft Rescue and Firefighting, along with gas and chemical expertise."

"Okay, but what does that have to do with me?" Kora looked around wildly, then had to stand to get away from the feeling of being boxed in. The others must have seen something on her face, because they quickly stood and backed away from her. She paced the area where Hank and Jake had been sitting, then looked over at Seth. "Talk."

Seth sighed heavily then looked at Jake.

"You were injured during the fire that covered up Chief Jade's murder," Jake began. "We asked the Falco brothers to join Fool's Gold FD to help us ferret out, not only his killer, but also the arsonist who set the fire to cover it up. Troy being an investigator over in Denver, we asked him to come, but he'd only come if his brothers joined him. I won't get into all those details, because they're not mine to tell, but we also hired them to help protect anyone that needs protecting."

"In addition to being a firefighter?" Kora looked at Seth as she asked that.

"Yes."

"Okay, but what does that have to do with me?" She scowled as the man she'd come to learn as Trent set her own helmet in the center of her desk.

Before she could question him, Jake continued, "When Troy and Esme began their investigation into Chief Jade's death, they handed copies of all their findings over to the Brotherhood Protectors. When we have the chance, one of us goes through the file to see if we can see anything that might have been missed."

"And?" Kora prompted when Jake remained silent.

This time it was Hank who answered, "And we found a letter threatening your life if you ever returned to work from your injuries. I won't beat around the bush here, Kora, what did you think earlier today when Seth knocked you to the ground and covered you?"

Kora shook her head in confusion. "No clue. One minute we were talking, the next I was on the ground, and he told me not to move. I was going to wait until everything calmed down here later, then go and talk to him about it." She turned toward Seth. "What did happen?"

"Someone shot at you." Seth didn't mince any words as he reached out and took her helmet off the desk and brought it to her. He pointed to a fresh, but deep scratch on the side of her helmet. "I heard the bark of the weapon, then this flew off your head. I dropped you to the ground to cover you, and afterward, Trent being an investigator, did his job." No one said a word when Trent tossed a small clear plastic bag on the desk, and Kora stared in shock when she saw a bullet inside.

"I recovered that from a few feet from where Seth dropped you to the ground. This was recovered in the area it was fired from." The second bag appeared, and it was the spent shell.

"Are you saying someone is trying to kill me?"

"We are," Jake said, and pulled a letter from his back pocket. Kora noted it was sheathed in yet another plastic bag. Jake looked between her and the letter in his hands several times, before asking, "Do you know a Darryl Trumbull?"

Kora frowned, then looked off to the side before she finally shook her head in confusion. "No, I've never heard that name before. Should I?"

"What did the letter say?" Kora asked as she crossed her arms over her middle, and felt her shoulders hunch, trying to make herself small. "Before you answer that, I have to say that I never suspected anything or anyone was after me when I was out of work."

"According to our investigation," Jake said as he looked between her and the papers he held. "The threat was *if* you returned to work. With today being your first day back, and someone took a shot at you, we are taking this threat against you very seriously. This means that someone is watching you. Not only is Seth working for Fool's Gold FD, he works for the Brotherhood Protection agency, and we hired him to look after you." He paused only long enough to catch his breath, then rushed forward. "As of right this minute, his Brotherhood task will be to keep you safe at all costs. He is to protect you. Kora, do not think that you don't need protecting. You do." He stressed the point as he lifted the papers, he had brought with him and shook them in the air.

"What aren't you telling me?" Kora frowned at her friend, as well as the others in the room. "I feel like you are leaving something important out. What is it?"

Jake looked at the other men in the room, then looked Kora directly in the eye. "Trumbull says that you only got your position as a Lieutenant because you slept with Chief Jade."

Before Kora could respond, Seth made a rude sound with his nose and throat, then looked at her with a scowl so hard, that Kora took a step back from him. "Figures."

"What's that supposed to mean?" Kora demanded.

"Since you slept with my old man, it's no wonder you slept with your former chief to get promoted."

"Crack!" Everyone stared in shock as they watched Kora's hand come up, slap Seth across the face, and his head was thrown back from the force of it. They also watched in horror as the impression of her hand began to form on the side of his face, leaving a bright red mark.

"I have never slept with anyone to get a job, especially not Shawn Falco," Kora bit out through gritted teeth, and she uncrossed her arms from her waist, then slammed her fisted hands on her hips, all the while glaring at Seth. "It abhors me that you would say something like that about my mentor and friend!"

Seth slammed his fisted hands on his hips and turned his glare onto Kora. "Ha! Shawn Falco was the biggest assholic bastard that walked the face of the earth. He would never willingly help anyone." He looked her up and down with a sneer. "Not unless he was getting something on the side." He quickly lifted his hand to grab her wrist when it looked like she was going to slap his face again.

"Assholic? Is that even a word?" Heath asked from behind him.

"No clue, we should look it up," Trent said.

"I like it even if it isn't a word," Troy admitted.

"I think it might be a word if Seth said it. With him being the oldest of us and more worldly, he would know," Marcus said.

Seth gritted his teeth, and with his hand still holding Kora's wrist, he threw his glare over his shoulder at his brothers, and caught the grins on their faces, as well as his employers. "Shut up," he ground out, then turned his attention back to the woman before him.

"When did you sleep with the old man? Was it

before or after you got promoted? Or was that when you slept with Chief Jade?"

"You son of a bitch, I never slept with anyone to get a promotion. Let go of me," she demanded, and jerked her hand from his, then took several steps back from him. She started to cross her arms around her middle and hunch into herself, but she had no reason to be ashamed, so she stood tall, lifted her head, and glared down her nose at him.

"You want to know the truth? Here's the truth. Shawn Falco was the best thing that ever happened in my life. He is my hero, and nothing you say or do will tell me otherwise."

Seth looked at her like she'd grown horns, and shook his head at her. "No way we're talking about the same man."

"Seth," Hank said from behind him. The tone of his voice indicated for Seth to look at him, but he didn't respond. "Maybe we should get Kora's side of the story, then we can get to the bottom of Trumbull's allegations."

"Fine," Seth said as he walked over to the wall, leaned his shoulder against it, and glared at Kora. "I'm listening. Convince me that Shawn Falco wasn't the assholic bastard he'd been all my life." He whipped his head over to his brothers, and bit out, "Can it." When they opened their mouths to comment. He turned back to Kora. "You can begin now."

CHAPTER 5

"I DON'T REALLY HAVE to tell you this, but I will, to prove to you what a wonderful man Shawn Falco was. Everything I'm about to tell you is on public record back in Denver if you doubt any of my story." She looked at him, then sighed heavily as she walked over to her desk, and picked up her coffee cup she'd set there earlier. She took a sip, then sighed again. "Please bear with me as I give you a little background of my life before I get to the point where Shawn became my hero."

She didn't wait for Seth or the others to respond, but glared when Seth made a rude remark. Ignoring the others in the room, she put all her focus on the man leaning against her office wall before she began.

"I had a good life growing up until I was eight. I had two parents, and a sister, we lived in a good neighborhood in Denver, and Mom and Dad had great jobs. I have no idea what happened, but things started to change when I was around seven. Dad lost his job, but we were still living in our home." Kora scrubbed her forehead and turned a confused frown onto Seth. "I have no clue what happened, or how, but suddenly Mom and Dad started fighting all the time. Neither of them would go to work, the beautiful house we lived in became messier and messier with each passing day. Then things would come up missing."

"Missing how?" Seth frowned at her as he saw the genuine confusion in her expression.

"First it was mine and Sadie's TVs from our room, then our handheld games. At first it wasn't that noticeable, not until the big TV from the family room disappeared, along with our game consoles, and our DVD players, and all our movies. It was very confusing for Sadie and me, the next thing I know, the police are there and taking Mom and Dad away in handcuffs, then someone else came and took Sadie and me away. We were told that our parents had done something wrong and had to go to jail, while we were being put into foster care. At first, we were together, and everything seemed to work, but then the emergency home we went to couldn't keep us long term, and they ended up splitting us up." Kora felt the anguish from that time creep up on her, but she beat it back with several deep breaths, and staring at Seth, focusing only on him. She hoped it would help her get through her story if she didn't have to concentrate on the others in the room. "Several weeks later, our case worker came to get me, they needed me to go live with Sadie."

"Why?" Seth scowled at her explanation.

"We didn't find out until months later, but Sadie started having seizures. I'll get to it, but it was Shawn that was able to get to the bottom of it. If I tell you now, it would be jumping ahead in the story. I want to tell this once, then put it back in its box in the back of my mind to never open again." She sighed and looked around the room, then continued, "As I said, Sadie started having seizures, and when I went to be with her, they stopped. Because of her health, we were able to stay together for the rest of our time in foster care. I know I'm rushing this, but I need to get it out. Anyway, we were in foster care for eighteen months before we were able to go home with Mom. It was the three of us for several months, then Dad got out of jail. Again, it wasn't until later that I found out they went to jail for drugs. When all the stuff started disappearing from our home, they sold it to buy their drugs. Mom got clean in jail, and came out with the determination of getting us girls back. It worked."

"And your father?" This time it was Hank who asked when she remained silent for so long.

"Dad was a different story," Kora sighed again as she shook her head to try to clear it. "It's hard to describe, but it seemed like when Dad got out of prison, he was strung out on drugs worse than when he went in. In case you're wondering, Mom served eighteen months, and Dad did two years. Because of Sadie's seizures, Mom refused to allow Dad back into our lives until he was completely clean. There were times when he'd show up higher than a kite, and things would get ugly between them. The police were always called, and they dragged Dad away in cuffs."

"What happened?" Seth asked when she paused in her story.

"One night Dad showed up unannounced. He was supposed to call ahead if he wanted to see Sadie or me. He showed up and began pounding on the door. Sadie was in the middle of a seizure when he broke the door down and rushed in." Kora stared off into space as she recalled what had happened that fateful night. "I was in the bathroom, Mom was in the living room with Sadie. I came down the hall and saw Mom trying to help Sadie, but Dad came up behind Mom and grabbed her by her hair and picked her up. I rushed forward to try to stop him, but he backhanded me and the knife he held in his hand sliced me." She reached up and unconsciously ran her hand over a spot on her collarbone and continued to stare into space, but she lowered the front of her tee a few inches and everyone saw the long white scar on her upper chest.

"When he backhanded me, he did it so hard that I flew across the room, and my head hit the door-frame to one of the bedrooms, then I blacked out."

"What happened next?" Seth asked, thinking he knew, but wanted her to tell him.

"A fireman was bending over me, and he took his facemask off and put it over my face. I remember his hands running up and down my arms and legs, then he picked me up and the next thing I remember is waking up in the hospital. It was three days later."

"Shit," Marcus said from behind her.

"How old were you?" Seth asked.

"Eleven, and it was Shawn Falco who found me and gave me his oxygen mask. He happened to be at the hospital trying to visit me when I woke, and he sat there and held my hand the entire time I told the police and the doctors what had happened. They were able to piece it all together."

"What?" Seth asked. This time he took two steps forward and took one of her hands in his. After giving it a gentle squeeze, he kept his attention on her. "What happened, Kora?"

"It turned out that Dad was higher than a kite

that night, and he wanted Mom to take him back. He wasn't taking no for an answer. His kicking in the door, screaming at Mom had set Sadie off, and because Mom ignored him to take care of her, he lost it. I tried to get Dad away from Mom, or Mom away from Dad, I'm not sure now, but after he swung out at me and sliced my chest, he killed Mom and set the apartment on fire. I have no clue whether he tried to save Sadie or not. All I know was that the man who saved me from that fire was there holding my hand when the police told me that both my mother and sister were dead."

"What about your father?" Seth asked.

"He disappeared, and wasn't found until six months later, with a needle stuck in his arm. They found him in a crack house during a routine bust."

"Shit," Seth said, and held her hands tighter.

"I remember that," Trent said as he looked at his brothers. "Remember? Dad said he had to go to a funeral for a little girl who had just lost her father. If this is what I remember, then this happened within a month of Seth leaving for the Marines."

Kora gave the month and date of her family's death, and watched Seth as he nodded.

"I left for the Marines two weeks before that date. Are you telling me that it was my old man that saved you from that fire?"

"Yes, he held my hand as I told my story to the police, and he was there again with the police when they told me about finding Dad's body, then again for his funeral. Over the years, Shawn would show up at my foster home four times a year."

"Which were?" Seth asked in confusion, trying to reconcile the man she described as the man he'd known as a father. It wasn't adding up.

"My birthday, Sadie's birthday, Mother's Day, and the anniversary date of when my mother and sister was buried. He said he was there to help me through it."

"What did he do?" Trent asked.

"With permission from my caseworker, and my foster parents, Shawn would pick me up at seven in the morning and we would spend the day together. Regardless of what day of the week it would fall on. If it was a school day, I still spent it with Shawn. We'd go to the park, a museum, a ball game, or just someplace to talk."

"How long did that last?" Seth asked.

"As I said, he picked me up at seven in the morning, but he never took me home until seven that night. We spent the entire day together. It started a year after the fire, and stopped when I moved here to Fool's Gold seven years ago." Kora smiled suddenly, and Seth had to suck in his breath at her beauty. "In all that time, there was only one time that we got in an argument, and he didn't show up on one of his four yearly visits." Kora shook her head, then looked around the room, feeling she had to explain. "That was on me, I told him not to show up, because I couldn't agree to what he proposed of me."

"Which was?" Seth asked through gritted teeth as he held his breath for her answer.

"When I was a senior in high school, I told Shawn I was going to become a firefighter as soon as a I graduated. He told me that he couldn't support that decision, and demanded that I go to college to get a degree. We had a gigantic fight over it. In the end, it turned out he was right, and I did go to college to get a degree. I don't know whether it pissed him off or not, but I got my degree in Fire Science." Kora said proudly, then looked at everyone in the room directly in the eye. She locked her eyes on Seth as she continued, "*That* was how I got my promotion, it sure as hell wasn't because I slept with Chief Jade. I got it because of that degree I took over twelve years ago. I also make sure that I'm up-to-date on any new things that I need to know."

Seth nodded, but didn't comment as he continued to stare at her.

"What?"

"I can't see our father being that nice to some-one. I can't speak for my brothers, but as I said, he was an assholic bastard to me almost my entire life. It was so bad, that was why I left home at the age of seventeen to join the Marines. I only got out about two months before he died."

"You never saw him all that time?"

"Nope, and because of my experience with him, don't feel sorry for me. He was a bastard, and I hated him. Though I never saw the old man, I kept in touch with my brothers, and that was how I knew about Heath."

"I don't understand."

"Let's table that discussion for another time," Hank said. "I don't like to delve too far into the personal lives of my employees, and I'll leave Seth to tell you when he's ready. Right now, I need to be someplace else, and we need to nail these details down." Hank's tone brooked no argument, and they all turned their attention to him.

"As I said, during the investigation of the fire where Chief Jade was murdered, we uncovered threats against you. They're only coming to light because you are back to work, and someone shot at you today. Being part of the Brotherhood, and because you will work closely with Seth, from this day forward, until this Trumbull guy is found, he will be your constant companion. While here in the firehouse, that should work perfectly. I'll leave it to the two of you to figure out who is moving in with whom when you're off duty."

"What?" Both Seth and Kora demanded. "What

do you mean who is living with whom? Are you saying that we have to live together?"

"Yes, how else is he going to protect you?" Hank grinned when the two people before him began sputtering, but he held up his hand to halt them. "Figure it out by yourselves, but, Garrison, Falco will be protecting you. Don't let me find out you gave him the slip, then something happened to you. I'm sure I don't have to tell you what RJ will do to Jake if that happens."

"Way to lay the guilt trip, Patterson," Kora said, then turned to Seth. "I only have a one-bedroom apartment."

"I have the ranch house, it has four spare rooms." Seth nodded, then turned to his brothers with a grin, ignoring Kora's sharp intake of breath. "That means you're going to have to go back to your own homes, boys." He laughed evilly at their moans, but only shook his head at them. "Talk to Charli. I'm sure I overheard her telling everyone at last night's supper that there was no reason why you still had to stay in my house. Isn't that right, Marcus?"

"Fine," the younger man said, and looked at his brothers. "Maybe we should go back to our houses and leave these two to get to know each other."

"Works for me," Troy said as he stood. "On that note, I'll let the two of you figure out the details. I have calls to make, and a department to run." He quickly left, but not before shaking Jake and Hank's hand, then he and the others left, leaving Seth and Kora alone. Kora did note that Jake had left a file on her desk, and she quickly nodded.

"I'll read over the file and see if anything triggers on the name of Trumbull for me. I'll then give it to you. We don't need to discuss our living arrangements outside this office while we're here on duty. What we do outside of working hours is no one's business but ours."

"I agree."

"Can we trust your brothers to keep their mouths shut?"

"I'll have a word with them."

"Okay, then here's my report for this morning's fire. I'll be in the kitchen." She started to walk away, but Seth stopped her.

"I thought you said you were going to read the file to see if you remembered Trumbull."

"I need to think, and I know women all over the world will shoot me for saying this, but I can think better if I'm cooking. I noticed that you're on the rotation for tonight's supper, would you mind if I cooked it instead?"

"Not at all, when I cook, I pay for the pizza to be delivered."

Kora didn't know whether he was joking or not, but his expression didn't seem like it was a joke, so she left it alone. "I'll be in the kitchen." She quickly walked out of her own office, and down the stairs to the room that was her salvation in the back of the firehouse. After looking in the refrigerator to see the supplies, she quickly got to work, trying not to think about going home with Seth at the end of her shift in two days.

CHAPTER 6

KORA PARKED her truck where Seth had told her to
less than an hour ago as they had prepared to leave
her apartment. After their conversation with Hank
and Jake, they had worked the rest of their shift,
and hadn't had any more fires other than the grass
fire on Friday. Having no fires caused the firefighters to get antsy, but Troy ran a tight ship, and
when they'd left that morning, every piece of
equipment and furniture in the house gleamed. It
helped that most of them were former military, and
were used to making sure everything was spit
shined. Now they had the next twenty-four hours
off, and Seth had followed Kora to her apartment
to get some clothes before taking her out to
Paradise Ranch on the outskirts of town.

"You don't lock your doors?" Kora asked as she
followed Seth up the stairs of his front porch, and

he opened the door and walked in, holding the door open for her.

"Nope," Seth, a man of few words said. She did note that he wasn't a typical guy who tossed his duffel on the floor beside the door. Instead, he told her to follow him, and he immediately emptied his bag into the washer. "Might as well add your clothes to mine, save on water." He stood there until she had added her dirty clothes, then started the washer. Next, he went down a short hall and through a doorway, and Kora stood in it and frowned.

"I know," Seth chuckled. "It's lacking flair, but the foundation is solid."

Kora giggled, "You do realize that the fifties are calling asking for their kitchen back?"

"Yep, when I bought the ranch, I bought it for its size and the outbuildings. I didn't much mind the inside. As long as the roof didn't leak, and it sat on a solid foundation, I didn't really care about anything else." As he explained, he had put together a pot of coffee, then stared at her with a raised brow. "I don't know about you, but I won't go to sleep until tonight. On my days off, I try to keep with the same routine, so I won't be exhausted when a call comes in, or wide awake when it's time to sleep."

"I agree," Kora said as she entered the kitchen, and took a seat over by the wall next to a phone with a long, twisty cord. "Does this still work?" She giggled her question, then gave a shriek of surprise when it rang.

"Yep," Seth said as he went over, picked up the receiver, then scowled at her. "Falco," he barked into it, and scowled even harder. "Whatever," he said and hung up. He glared at her before going back to what he had been doing, which was waiting for the coffee to finish.

"What's wrong?"

"Nothing, why?"

"Because, you scowled at me as you mumbled on the phone, then you hung up on whoever you were talking to." Kora looked up in shock as several people began to file into the house from what she assumed was the back. Not only was it the men she'd just spent the weekend working with, but three women entered also. Introductions were quickly made, and she was glad she sat against the wall, out of the way.

"My family," Seth said at one point as he brought Kora a cup of coffee. "Likes to cook breakfast here. God only knows why, because as you can see, this kitchen isn't really up-to-date and modernized."

Before any of Seth's siblings could say anything, Kora said, "It feels like home. Family."

"Excuse me?" At her words everyone turned to

look at her with different expressions, but the consensus was shock or surprise.

"What do you mean?" Heath asked as he paused with a stack of plates in his hands.

"I've only been here for less than twenty minutes, but the way you guys walked in the back door and immediately helped out, knowing where everything is, and the dancing around each other speaks to me like you've been doing this all your lives. That you're used to having the others underfoot, and you did it growing up. You know, like a family, and now you're doing it here, in your own home, or rather Seth's home. I saw it at the station, I thought it was a work thing, but it's not." Her words caused the others to stop and stare at her. "What did I say wrong?"

As one, four men and three women turned to look at Seth, and he stood there with a shell-shocked look on his face. It was Esme who hurried over to him, took the spatula from his hand, and guided him to a chair, which Kora had to hop out of to let him sit. No one said a word as they continued to get breakfast cooked, setting food on platters, then carried into the dining room. There was no table large enough in the kitchen for them to use. Kora was directed to sit to Seth's right, and she noted that he sat at the head of the table. No one said a word as they filled their plates and began eating. Once they were almost done, Seth pushed his plate away from him, crossed his arms in front of him on the table, then leaned in and looked at everyone. No one said a word as he began talking.

"When I first looked into buying this ranch, I had every intention of bringing us brothers together again. It was a goodwill gesture on my part."

"Why?" Kora frowned at him as she looked at the others, and noted they hung on Seth's every word, especially his brothers.

Seth leaned back in his chair with a fresh cup of coffee and looked around the room. "I can't speak for my brothers, and I won't, but from my perspective, growing up with the old man was hell. I couldn't wait to get the fuck out of the house." He looked over at his brothers and shrugged. "Sorry."

"Don't be," Trent said. "We knew Dad was especially hard on you, but we could never understand why."

"I'm the baby of the family," Marcus said. "I wasn't even five when you left, and I knew there was bad blood between you and Dad."

"I was the 'oops' that showed up at the door after you left, and even I felt the tension in Dad whenever one of us spoke your name," Heath admitted.

"He never asked after you," Troy admitted. "We always told him what you had been up to after we received a letter, or an e-mail, or after we met you on leave."

It was several minutes before anyone spoke again, and this time it was Kora who broke the silence. "I don't understand. Shawn was such a wonderful man, and such a great father figure, so why do you guys hate him so much?"

Her statement was met with utter silence, until Seth leaned forward again and began,

As I said a couple of days ago at the station, Shawn Falco was an assholic bastard." He covered his smirk when his future sisters-in-law began talking.

"Assholic?"

"Is that even a word?"

"We'll have to look it up." He grinned at them, and they swallowed and stared at their men in confusion.

"He's scaring us," Esme said to Troy. "I don't know if I like that grin or not." Her statement caused the others to burst out laughing, and it eased the building tension.

Seth took pity on them and began talking, but he directed his attention to Kora. "I don't know if you know this, but I am the oldest of this lot," he chuckled as he extended his arm to encompass everyone at the table. "Oh, not the ladies, they're dating my brothers. In case no one said anything to you earlier, here's the line-up. Esme is with Troy, Charli is with Marcus, and Tessa is with Heath."

Kora looked around the table and nodded at the couples when they nodded back to her. She noted that they had stacked the dishes at the end of the table and didn't make any moves to leave the conversation. As she studied them, she realized they were hanging onto Seth's every word. She wondered if he was as quiet in his personal life as he had been at the station. He only talked when asked a direct question, or when it came to his job as being Captain of the firehouse. She turned back and did the same as the others, waiting for him to continue.

"Where to start?"

"Wherever you want," she said, then because it felt right, she reached out and covered his hand with hers, not knowing if it was surprise or acceptance when he turned his hand and entwined their fingers.

While looking at nothing but the table before him, he began again, "Before the age of seven, living with the old man wasn't so bad. There was Mom, the old man, me, and the twins, Troy and Trent. I think I was around five and the twins had just started walking when Grandpa moved in with us."

"Really? We were that young?" Troy asked. "I remember him, but barely."

"Yes, I remember overhearing an argument

between Mom and the old man. She wanted to know how she was supposed to take care of three children, and an old man when her husband was never home. Based on that conversation, it was either have Grandpa come live with us, or go into a home. He didn't have the insurance or extra money for a home, so Shawn decided to convert our screen-in porch into a bedroom for his father."

"What happened?" Kora asked when she felt him tense.

"First, it worked well, Grandpa had been a fireman all his life, and then he became sick, but it wasn't like he was bedridden sick. He could still walk around and do things around the house. We all know that their insurance, well, it's good, it's not great. Anyway, no one knew what was wrong with him, but if he didn't use oxygen, he couldn't really do anything."

"What do you mean no one knew what was wrong with him?" Heath asked.

"As I said, he had breathing problems, but he didn't have lung cancer, he didn't have COPD, or anything like that, he just had trouble breathing."

"Fireman's lung," Kora said, and everyone turned to stare at her. "That's what the man I replaced at the station years ago retired from. That's what they called it, you had trouble breathing, but there was no medical explanation for it." She looked around the table and nodded at Esme.

"It was the retiring chief before your dad came to the station."

"Ah, I vaguely remember him."

"Anyway," Seth said after a few minutes of silence. "Grandpa would work on the porch while Dad was at the station." He looked at Kora and explained. "We lived in Denver at the time. Life was good, I liked our little family. Then one night, it all blew up, literally, and nothing was the same afterward." No one said a word as they waited for Seth to continue. He drew in a deep breath and let it out slowly before he did. "I was seven, the twins were four, we had just had our bath, Mom had read to us and put us down for the night. Shawn was on duty, and Grandpa was working on the porch. See, he had taken over my room until it could be completed, but with Shawn working a lot, Grandpa could only do so much."

"I remember that," Troy said. "I remember having to share a bed with Trent, because you moved into our room."

"That was because Grandpa needed a room." Seth nodded, then looked at the table, and Kora could tell he was remembering that night. No one said a word as they waited for him to tell them what had happened. They'd been waiting for a long time for him to tell them what exactly occurred to make him hate their father so much.

"Mom came running into our room and she

woke me. She told me there was a fire and that I was to get the twins out." He looked over at Kora and gave a sad smile. "Being children from a family of firefighters, we knew the escape route from every room, and where to meet once we were out. There was an empty lot half a block away, and that was where we were to meet. I had enough time to throw on a pair of shoes, and I grabbed the twins and carried them down the stairs and out the door. I set them down, see I made them carry their own shoes as I carried them. I told them to put them on, and I rushed back into the house to help Mom and Grandpa. Mom screamed at me to get the twins to safety. I told her they were outside, she came to me, took my face in her hands, and practically screamed at me to get them to the lot. She would go get Grandpa and meet us there. I saw Grandpa coming up the hall behind her, and knew they would make it. I kissed her cheek, then turned and ran outside." He paused and Kora didn't say anything when his grip on her hand tightened. She did glance over and saw his brothers hanging on every word he said. "As soon as I ran back out of the house, I heard the sirens coming and all I could think was that everything was going to be okay, because Dad was on his way. I picked up Troy and Trent, and ran as fast as my legs could carry me. We were almost at the lot when we were thrown to the ground from the explosion."

"Oh, shit," Kora said, and tightened her grip.

"Yeah," Seth didn't say anything for several minutes, then he drew in a gigantic breath and let it out in a rush. "I picked the three of us up, and hurried down to that lot we were supposed to meet in. Several of our neighbors were there. It was a long time before Shawn arrived. I kept waiting to see Mom and Grandpa come through the smoke and be with us, but it never happened.

"The fire was out, and the police were there talking with the witnesses, and that's when Shawn arrived. He immediately went to the firemen to get their story, then when he finally arrived at the lot, he grabbed Troy and Trent and gathered them in his arms. I'll never forget what he said, and because of his statement, that was the day I started hating him, and he became the assholic bastard to me."

"What did he say?" Kora held her breath as she saw the anguish in his face when he looked at her.

"He looked down his nose at me, and with each twin in his arms, he told me that it was my fault Mom and Grandpa were dead. I was the oldest child and the man of the house when he wasn't there, and it had been my responsibility to get everyone else out."

"Fuck me," Trent said as he sighed heavily and looked at his twin.

"Yeah, what he said. I don't remember him saying that, but I do remember the resentment and hatred between the two of you after that. It seemed to get worse as we grew up."

"Yeah, it turned out that the older I got, the more I looked like Mom, the more the old man resented me. He even told me that it was too hard to look at me, because I looked like her, and it was my fault she was dead. He even would go so far as to call me a murderer. The only relief I got was from Loraine."

"Who is she?" Kora demanded, and hadn't realized she sounded jealous until she saw the grins on the others' faces.

"My mom," Marcus said. "Dad remarried, and I am the result of that second marriage. Before Mom passed, she told me that while Seth had been in the house, it was like living with a ghost and the tension was always high between her and Dad." Marcus looked at Seth and held up his hand. "It wasn't you. I made sure she didn't feel that way about you. It was Dad. She told me it was like living with the ghost of his dead wife when you were around."

The rest of them remained silent, until Seth sighed heavily and continued his tale. "Everything with the old man came to a head about a month before I left for the military." He looked around and saw he had everyone's attention. "I was out with friends, and I saw the old man through the window of a restaurant." He looked at Marcus apological. "It wasn't your mom. I saw red."

"What did you do?" Troy asked.

"I stormed across the street, went inside and right up to the table. The old man didn't see me at first, I came up behind him, but I stood there and stared at the woman."

"Oh, shit," Trent whispered. "What did you say? Because you wouldn't confront anyone without saying what was on your mind."

"I ignored the old man and flat-out told the woman that he was married, and had four kids at home." Seth looked at Heath then, "Sorry, we didn't know about you then."

"Don't be," Heath said as he waved his concern off. "What happened next?"

"The old man sputtered and tried to say I was the neighborhood jokester, but I wouldn't back down. I looked at the woman and told her all our names and where we lived. The old man tried to duck walk me out of the restaurant, but on the way out, I saw someone that knew us and called out across the dining room for him to talk to the woman Shawn was with." Seth paused as he sipped his coffee, then looked around the table with a grin. "All hell broke loose when we got outside."

CHAPTER 7

"OH, SHIT, WHAT HAPPENED?" Troy asked as he chuckled at Seth, then looked around the table at his brothers. Kora saw they all had leaned forward and waited with bated breath to hear what he had to say.

"The friends I was with before I entered that restaurant had the foresight to call the sheriff, and he was just pulling up when we exited the restaurant. The old man shoved me against the side of the building, pulled his arm back like he was going to hit me, but the sheriff was right there to stop him. He knew us, and he told the old man if he did hit me, he would have to arrest him, because I was underage."

"You don't call him Dad, or your father, do you?" Kora asked in shock.

"Nope, I'll get to that. With the old man being

restrained by the sheriff, who had to cuff him to keep him away from me, the woman came out and demanded to know what was going on. I tried to tell her the bastard was married, but he started screaming at me and calling me a liar. It was the sheriff that cleared up the matter after he put the old man in the back of his squad car. After that conversation, it turned out he had been seeing her for several months, and that was the night they were supposed to be having sex for the first time." Seth grinned when his brothers hooted out in laughter and made comments that he had cock-blocked their father.

"What happened next?" Kora had removed her hand from Seth's and sat back in her seat, trying to wrap her head around the man Seth had described to the man she knew. They were as different as night and day. She couldn't wrap her head around the man they were describing. Without saying a word, she continued to listen to the story as it unrolled.

"The sheriff had removed the old man from the back of the car, but didn't uncuff him, when the woman demanded answers, he only shrugged and said he wanted something new. She slapped him across the face and stormed off." Seth tried to wipe the grin off his face, but wasn't successful. "The manager came out of the restaurant then and demanded the bill to be paid. The sheriff uncuffed him long enough for him to get his wallet, then after that was taken care of, he told us both to meet him down at the station."

"Why you?" Heath asked. "Dad, I could understand, but you didn't do anything wrong."

"That's what I said," Seth nodded at them. "When I asked, the sheriff said he wanted us to iron out our differences and he didn't want to be called out to a murder scene, so we were going to the station to get everything out in the open." He shook his head, then settled back in his own seat. "The sheriff followed me the entire way, leaving the old man's truck at the restaurant."

"He was still cuffed in the back seat?" Kora asked in shock.

"Yep," Seth laughed. He quickly sobered, and looked around the table. "The old man screamed at me that he hated me, because I had killed his wife and father, then he shut up. I never said a word, and he refused to look at me. We sat there in silence for almost two hours before either of us spoke. I was the one to break the silence, but that was only after I had made a phone call. No, I wasn't under arrest, no, I wasn't cuffed like the old man, but I needed to get my point across."

"Who did you call?" Kora asked.

"The recruiter I'd been talking to from the Marine Corps, because I was only seventeen, he said I needed a parent's signature. He arrived, and with him standing beside me, I told the old man that I had the perfect way that he would never see me again. If he signed the papers, then I would be out of his hair in three days or less, and that would be the end of it."

"Did he give you any hassle?" Charli asked.

"He couldn't sign fast enough. As soon as the sheriff took the cuffs off, he grabbed the papers and signed. When he handed them back to the recruiter, he looked at me and told me he never wanted to see me ever again, not after murdering his wife and father." Seth sighed heavily and rubbed the back of his neck. "I had already explained the fire to the recruiter, and he looked into it. I looked my sperm donor dead in the eye and stood to my full height at that time. Being only seventeen I hadn't fully matured, but I was already two inches taller than him. I informed him that he would never see me again, and I would never call him the 'd' or 'f' word again. I turned on my heel and left. I have no clue what the recruiter or sheriff said to my father, but three days later I climbed on the bus and headed to Parris Island."

"What about your education?" Kora asked in shock. "Didn't you have to finish school?"

"That was the good thing. Dad hated me so much he never paid any attention to me. He would tell anyone who listened that I was a fuck up and that I wouldn't amount to anything. Because he hated me so much, and ignored me, I was able to double up on my classes. I talked to the guidance counselor when I entered the ninth grade, and we worked out a plan. I knew back then I wanted to join the Marines, and I worked my ass off to get out of school a year earlier to join."

"Holy shit, is that why you were always in summer school?" Troy asked in shock. "It was to take more classes, and not because you failed?"

"Correct, if anyone would have bothered to pay attention, they would have known I had a three point nine six grade point average. I didn't go out for the sports, because I didn't have the time, I was always studying."

"Is that why you didn't date either?" Marcus asked. He looked at the twins with a grin. "I remember these two always talking about girls, but never you. Not that I was very old when you left, but I never recalled you having a girlfriend."

"I didn't. Since the age of seven when the old man told me it was my fault my mother and grandfather were dead, I had the single focus of getting the fuck out of that town. I got the idea of joining the Marines from one of my teachers. He had been a former Marine and we talked excessively about it. If it wasn't for him, I don't know what I would have done. Sadly, he passed away a couple of years ago, so I can't go and tell him how I turned out."

Everyone remained silent for several moments

as they reflected on what Seth had said about his treatment from their father. Kora still couldn't wrap her head around what he had said. "I still can't see it," she said as she leaned forward and looked at Seth. "The man you described is not the man I knew."

"Believe it," all the men said. "We have our own stories of our experiences with dear old dad," Heath said. "I won't get into it, but when I first arrived on the scene, he called me a liar and told me that he wasn't my father. It took months of me showing up before he would admit that he was."

"Yeah," Seth shook his head at Heath's statement. He looked over at Kora to explain, "When I found out about Heath, since I was already in the military by then, and Troy sent me a letter telling me we had another brother, I reached out to Heath and asked for information."

"What type of information?"

"Who my mother was, where did I grow up, what was my actual birth date, shit like that," Heath answered for him. "I didn't hear back from him for almost six months, but since that first meeting, we've been brothers ever since."

"Why?" Kora asked. "Why did you need or even want that information?"

"Because I wanted to check up on something, and anything I could hold over the old man was sweet justice to me." He looked at his brothers, and nodded once. "I came back home once."

"No, you didn't," the others said, and when they saw his expression, Trent asked. "What did you do?"

"First, I asked a Marine buddy of mine to research all the information Heath gave me. It came back legit. Then I came home and armed with the information from him, I had called ahead of time and asked that the old man be kept away from the fire station."

"Oh, shit," Troy whispered.

"Yeah, because the fire was public record, and some of the old man's buddies still worked there, I did some investigating on my own. I was twenty-two, so he couldn't deny me anything, I was a legal adult. I talked to the former chief, and he was the one that told me what exactly happened in that fire."

"Which was?" Kora asked when no one else seemed to be able to speak.

"Yes, our house caught on fire, but remember me telling you that the old man and grandpa were converting a screened-in porch for grandpa's bedroom?"

"Yes, what?" Kora chuckled. "Was it faulty wiring?"

"It was," Seth didn't hesitate to answer, and this time he looked directly at Charli. "The wiring the old man purchased at a deep discount price turned out to be recalled because there were broken wires inside."

"Oh, shit, that's not good." Charli looked at Kora. "I'm a contractor. If there is broken wires inside the tubing if they spark, no matter how much insulation there is on the outside, there's almost a guarantee of an electrical fire. You're saying your father purchased the faulty wiring?"

"Yes, at least according to his old boss he did. That's what started the fire. After I got the twins out and tried to go back inside, Mom told me to take them to the lot, that she would get Grandpa. He had fallen asleep in the new, but now quite finished room where the fire started. Instead of turning off the oxygen or pulling his portable take with him, he took off the hose and threw it behind him. He was outside the room in the hall, and heading to the front door when the fire caused the oxygen tank to blow. He and Mom were found less than ten feet from the front door." No one said a word as they pictured what he had described. All the men and Kora were firefighters, and knew what it was like to encounter a dead body in a fire. It wasn't a pretty sight.

To steer their thoughts away from that image, Kora asked, "What did you do with the information?"

"While still home, I called the old man. Told him

that I knew what he had done the night of the fire, and it was him, not me, that killed his wife and father."

"How do you figure that?" Kora demanded.

"Because, when he didn't arrive at that lot until the fire was almost out, it was a three-alarm fire, he immediately jumped down my throat about it being my fault. He projected his guilt onto me."

"What guilt?"

"The night of the fire, when he wasn't there, he had been at Heath's place spending time with him and his mother."

"That was the last time I saw him." Heath admitted. "For years when I would tell my mother that I remember a man reading to me, she said it was my imagination. Before she died, she came clean and told me the truth, that the man I remembered was my father, but something happened, and they broke it off."

"In case you haven't figured it out yet," Seth said as he looked at Kora. "Heath is younger than I am, but older than the twins."

"I am the result of an affair that Shawn Falco had."

Kora sat there stunned, not knowing what to think of all the information that they had revealed about her hero and mentor.

It was silent for a long time, until Tessa spoke for the first time, "Not to be nosy or anything, but who are you, and what are you doing here?" She looked directly at Kora when she asked.

"Oh," Kora said, and looked at Seth for a way of explanation. They never did say what they would tell his family about her being in his home.

"I'm protecting her." Seth came right out and said it. "Jake and Hank came to the station on Friday and told us that they were investigating something from the fallout of your father's death, Esme." He looked at her and saw her sit up and pay closer attention.

"What's that?"

"It was a letter they received around that time, but was put on the back burner, it wasn't until another letter came in that they started to pay attention. We knew nothing about it, and on Friday after we all did our recertification physicals, we were called out for a grass fire."

"And?" the women asked when he paused.

"And someone tried to shoot Kora. I shoved her to the ground and covered her, while the others made sure she was safe getting back to the truck. Trent stayed back and investigated. He was able to find the shell and the slug. Kora has a new groove in her helmet where the bullet grazed her."

"Holy hell." Tessa looked at her in shock. "You're here so Seth can protect you?"

"I am. I have no clue what this person wants

from me, or even who he is. I've never heard of him before."

"What's his name?" Charli asked.

"It's some guy by the name of Darryl Trumbull."

"Well, there's a classic assholic bastard if there ever was one," Esme said, and watched as everyone turned to look at her with varying degrees of anger and shock.

CHAPTER 8

"You know him?" Kora sat up quickly, and demanded of the woman sitting on the other side of the table. "How? Who is he? Why does he have it out for me?"

"What do Jake and Hank say?" Esme asked Seth.

"Nothing much, just that they received a letter stating that Kora only got her position by sleeping with your father. That was the first letter. The second one stated if she was allowed to return to work, then there would be hell to pay. They were on their way to us to tell us that bit of information while we were out fighting that brush fire."

"That's when Kora was shot at?"

"It was."

Esme began stacking the dishes in front of her, and Kora could tell she was trying to gather her thoughts. She did the same with her and Seth's dishes, as did the other women. No one said a word as they were carried into the kitchen and then they all cleaned up. As much as Kora wanted to take Esme by the shoulders, shake her, and shout at her, she knew she wouldn't be able to force any answers from her. It was almost an hour before they all settled back down at the dining room table with a fresh cup of coffee and at least three carafes full sitting in the middle of the table.

"What do you know?" Kora finally asked, trusting the woman she'd known since coming to work at the Fool's Gold firehouse seven years prior. Though she wasn't best friends with her, she had known her from when she'd come into the station to have a word with her father, Chief Jade, who had been murdered, and the killer had set the fire to cover it up.

"I'd have to refer to my notes, but I can give you a rough estimate of a timeline for what I know."

"We can work with that," Seth said. "Whatever you have, it will help us out. Just by your expression you have more information than Jake and Hank. We can always go back to them with whatever you have and get it verified."

"Okay, I can work with that." Esme drew in a deep breath and let it out slowly. "Darryl Trumbull is a tool. He thinks he's more important than he is, and he's borderline at his job."

"What do you mean by that?" Kora asked in confusion.

"This is from a conversation I had with Dad before you even came to Fool's Gold. So, we're talking years ago when I wasn't a fire investigator yet. I remember we were sitting at the table eating, and he and Mom were talking about the list of new recruits that were applying to the station. He never got into specifics with Mom and me, unless he had a hard decision to make, and he had always been able to talk them out with Mom."

"What did he say?"

"He was telling us about the new people he wanted to hire, and he leaned heavily in your direction. You came highly recommended for the job, and hired you because of your scores, your work ethics, your reputation, and your overall personality. I think what tipped the final scales in your favor were the letters of recommendation not only from Shawn Falco, but also from your former chief. Dad hired you."

"And Trumbull? What about him? Because I can tell you right now that I have absolutely no clue who he is."

"You might not because he wanted to transfer to Fool's Gold from Colorado Springs. When Dad asked him why, he said because he wanted to, and I'm quoting Dad here, 'rest on his laurels, and not have to work as hard as expected of him.' Unquote."

"Holy shit, he really said that?" Troy asked in shock.

"He did. I know it's all hearsay on my part, but I have never forgotten that conversation in all these years. That statement always stuck with me and when Dad sent him the rejection letter, he showed up at the fire station and wanted to know how long he had been sleeping with Kora, because that was the only way a woman would be hired over him. He kept spouting off that he was the best of the best, but got really, I mean extremely pissed off when Dad called him out on a few things."

"Like?" Kora asked, and noted Seth had leaned forward and was paying rapt attention to what Esme had to say.

"Like during his recertification physical he had to take it over three times. He was over the seven-minute mark by thirty seconds the first time, fifteen seconds the second time, and two seconds the third time. He barely squeaked by with four tenths of second to spare the fourth time he took it. His file from Colorado Springs had some write-ups where he wasn't a team player both in the fire-house and at the scene of the fires. I remember one quote was that he tried to be a hotshot and throw his weight around at the scene, and tried to order his own Chief, Captain, and Lieutenant around."

"Wow," Kora said as she leaned back in her

chair. She frowned, then looked at Esme in confusion. "Did he ever take his Lieutenant's exam?"

"He did, again, he failed it several times and has to wait for three years before he can take it again. He failed it that many times."

"Can I ask something?" Tessa held up her hand to draw attention to them.

"What's that?" Seth asked.

"Is this guy stable, I mean mentally?" As she asked, she took her forefinger and tapped her own temple. "If he felt Kora took his job away from him, not only way back when in order to come to Fool's Gold, but what about when she became a Lieutenant? Does anyone know what he does now?"

"Last I heard," Esme said, and saw everyone staring at her. "Last I heard, he'd been hurt in the fire where they found Dad's body and was out on medical leave. I can't tell you the extent of his injuries, or whether he's even back to work yet."

"I'll start there," Seth said as he pushed his chair back and stood. "Not that I don't enjoy you guys here in my home, but I have work to do. You know the way out." The others laughed, and when Troy saw Kora's shocked expression at the abruptness of Seth's leaving, he laughed harder.

"That's Seth, man of very few words, but when he does say something we all hang onto what he says, because we know it to be the absolute truth. Things he said earlier about how Dad treated him, we knew it was something, but never the exact details. I can see our father saying those things to him. I'm sorry it that bursts your bubble when it comes to Shawn Falco, and I'm not being a bastard about it. You only saw him four times a year, we saw him every day all day for years. We all joined the military to get away from him."

Kora watched as the others cleaned up the coffee cups, and headed toward the kitchen, she followed, not knowing what to do with herself after they left. To keep herself busy, she cleaned all the counters, then went to the laundry room and put the clothes they'd tossed in the washer earlier into the dryer and turned it on. With nothing else to do, she decided to raid the refrigerator, not that she was hungry, but she wanted to see if she should cook anything.

"Didn't you get enough to eat?" Seth said from behind her, causing Kora to jump with a little scream.

"What the hell, Falco?" She glared at him, then when she saw the gigantic grin on his face, she didn't know whether to slap him or beg him to take her to bed. It had been a long time since she'd been with a man, and this man before her was the most handsome she'd ever seen in a long, long time. She gave herself a mental slap and stepped back from him. Just because she was living in his house until they could find the person who had shot at her a few days ago, didn't mean she could jump his bones. Besides, they worked together, and there was no way she would put her job in jeopardy to scratch an itch.

"What's up?" she asked, to turn the conversation back onto him.

"I put a call into Jake with the information Esme gave us. He said he'd look into it and get back to me." Seth scowled at her expression of shock. "What?"

"You're going to let someone else tell you how to do your job?"

"What's that supposed to mean?"

"It means that you should be the one to look into things. What if Jake sees something that he doesn't think is relevant? Does he know what it's like to be a firefighter? Does he know what to look for in Trumbull's record? Something that he might ignore, or overlook would be a glaring red flag to either of us. I don't know about you, but I don't want someone who doesn't know the work we do to be in control of the information we need to take this guy down. We, or rather, I, was lucky the bullet only grazed my helmet. I'll be honest here, Seth, if it wasn't for you throwing me to the ground and covering me, I would have picked up my helmet and put it back on my head, having no clue what had happened."

"What are you saying?" Seth asked as he

dumped the contents of the coffee cup, he'd taken to his office with him and didn't see her roll her eyes behind his back at the question. He turned with a smirk, he only raised a brow at her.

"Sorry, not sorry, but if I was conducting this investigation, the first thing I would do would be to get my hands on Trumbull's file." When he didn't immediately put the kibosh on her suggestion, she drew in a deep breath and let it out quickly as she warmed to her idea. "I'm a Lieutenant, and I have some pull, but not in a different house. You're a Captain, and you have more pull than I do, again, I don't think you'd have that much pull with the Colorado Springs firehouse." She paused then frowned at him. "Do you know of any firefighters from there?"

Seth stared at her, but Kora could tell that he wasn't really seeing her, so she waited him out, when his expression cleared, he looked directly at her, causing her to suck in her breath at how handsome he was. "I met a couple of them when we fought the wildfire last month."

"Do you know them well?"

"They invited me out for a drink when I had the time. I haven't taken them up on it yet."

"Do it," Kora said, and in her excitement, she reached out and took his hand in hers, and they both jumped and jerked at the shock of skin-on-skin contact. Instead of dropping his hand, she squeezed tighter and stared into his eyes. She grinned when his eyes flared, but they both dropped their hands and stepped back.

"We can't," Seth said as he took several steps away from her.

"I know. I don't mean to tell you what to do, but if you felt something when I grabbed your hand, and we can't do anything about it, then you best go call whoever you met at that wildfire and set up a meeting with them. The faster we find out if Trumbull is the guy behind shooting at me, the faster we can take him out, allowing me to get on with my life and out of your hair. There is no way we can do anything with us working in the same fire station."

"I agree," Seth said as he took several more steps away from her. "I'll go call him, I have his card in my office."

"In the meantime, what can I do around here?"

Seth's face broke out into a gigantic grin, causing Kora's brows to lift.

"What?" she asked tentatively, not liking his expression of evil glee.

"Do you like flowers?"

"I do, what does that have to do with anything?"

"There are some flowers growing outside, and the women said I need to weed them, I have no clue which is a flower, and which is a weed. They won't let me mow them over, they yell at me all the time, then the men yell at me for yelling back." He hung his head and sighed. The look he gave her was like a little lost boy, and she fell hard for him right there in his kitchen. "If you could start to weed my flowers, I can come out and help you."

"Sure, get me started with some things and I'll meet you outside." Together they went out and he took her to a shed that held all his gardening supplies. After he showed her those, he took her to the areas where they could see the flowers. Kora waved him off and went back to the shed, while he went inside to make his call. He came back quicker than she anticipated, and she frowned at him. "Problem?"

"Yes, I do have that guy's card in my desk, however, it's in my desk at the station. The next time we're on is only for twenty-four, why don't I give him a call when we get in tomorrow and see if I can't hook up with him after our shift. If we're lucky, we can be on the same shifts."

"Sounds good, however, I have one quick question."

"Which is?"

"While you're protecting me, am I in your pocket twenty-four seven?"

"What do you mean? Of course, I'll be with you at all the time."

"Will we be driving into work together?"

"Tell me what you're thinking, then we can discuss it."

When Kora didn't say anything, Seth reached down and took her hands in his, and when he felt the shock again, he tightened his grip on her fingers, not allowing her to pull away from him. "Kora, for this protection thing to work, we're going to have to learn to trust each other. If you need to be someplace, then I will get you there, but I won't allow you to go alone."

Kora studied his face, then sighed heavily. "Fine, but don't be mad at me."

"What is it, Kora?"

"Since I was injured and had to stay home, I started feeding some stray cats that started hanging out in the alley behind my apartment." She looked at him and smirked at his expression and wrinkled her nose at him. "I know, it was a bad idea because they're wild or whatever, but I couldn't see them starving."

"Did you try to catch any of them?"

"I did." She took her hands from his and lifted her left arm to point to the inside of her forearm. Seth leaned in close to get a look at the fine white scars, and Kora closed her eyes to draw in a lungful of his fragrance. "I wasn't successful. We came to an agreement," she laughed. "As long as I fed them, they would occasionally allow me to pet them."

"How often?" Seth smirked.

"Three times since this happened." She indi-cated her forearm again, then looked at him. "I won't stop feeding them, but I know I can't catch them either." She sighed as she stepped back. "That's all I want while I'm here, to leave a little bit earlier than you normally would to swing by and feed them."

"What about your days off?"

"I'll drive in and feed them. This way, I can gather my mail, and check out the apartment. I don't know about you, but I don't want it to appear that I'm not at home, you know? Make it look like I'm there in and out at odd hours. In case Trumbull is watching my apartment or something."

Seth studied her for a long time before he nodded. "I agree. I never gave it a thought about your mail, and it would look suspicious if all of a sudden, your mail begins to pile up, and your truck is gone." They continued to stare at one another before Kora broke the eye contact and sighed. In no time, Kora was settled into the task of weeding Seth's garden.

CHAPTER 9

SETH WALKED up the stairs later that night, bone-ass tired. After showing Kora the shed with the gardening tools, he had decided to bring out the lawn mower to tackle his lawn he should have mown a week ago. One thing had led to another, and after doing the riding mower, he brought out the weed eater to get all the trim work done. When he thought he was done with his lawn, Heath had come over and asked for his help on a project, and all the brothers had come to help before moving on to another project at Trent's place. Now he wanted a shower before he had to start dinner, which he wasn't looking forward to. He hoped one of his brothers had brought something over for him and Kora during the day. He sure couldn't ask her to cook for them, it wouldn't seem right. Seth wasn't paying any attention as he strode down the hallway toward his room, and because he'd done it almost every night since moving into the house, he removed his shirt as he walked down the hall.

"Oof," came a voice, and Seth stumbled as he ran into someone. He quickly lowered his arms and grabbed whoever it was, and did some fancy footwork so they wouldn't go down in a heap in the middle of the hallway. He jerked the tee the rest of the way off, and stared down at Kora, who had one hand holding the towel wrapped around her hair, and another hand was clamped at her chest, trying to keep that towel in place. With his hands on her hips, he was able to feel where the towel had come loose and her entire backside was bare.

"Hey," he smirked down at her and grinned at her scowl. He moaned as his hands came into contact with bare, wet skin, causing him to freeze when she moaned as he massaged the area his hands made contact with, which happened to be her ass. When he saw her eyes flare, and she licked her lips, he became hard, making sure to grind himself against her lower stomach.

"What are you doing?" Kora asked as she continued to scowl at him. "Were you standing out here waiting for me? Why do you have your shirt off?"

Before she could get even more upset, he leaned

down and kissed her nose. "I think you missed a spot." He didn't allow her to say a word before he took his dirty hand and lifted it to rub one filthy finger across the top of her breasts, leaving a small line of dirt behind. He had a grin a mile wide when she looked at him, and instead of the scowl he expected, she smirked at him.

"Funny how I must have missed that spot," she sighed as she looked at him. Seth didn't know who acted first, and if he would have been brought in to testify in a court of law, he would have to say that this next step was unclear to him. As he watched the line of dirt he had just left across the top of Kora's breasts, her towel slipped, or was pulled down, exposing almost all of her. The only thing holding it up was her arm beneath her breasts.

"You need a shower," Seth said as he bent down and picked her up, and carried to the rest of the way down the hall to his bedroom. Without saying another word, they were suddenly in his newly installed bathroom, and he set her on the counter. Again, without saying a word, he quickly turned on the water, and stripped down to his birthday suit. With his hands on his waist, he turned to look at Kora, and smirked when he found her eyes zeroed in on his manhood.

"Eyes up here, lady," he laughed when her head jerked up, and she hit the back of it on the mirror behind her. He continued to chuckle when it looked like she was having trouble swallowing.

"I'm going to be blunt here, Kora. I want you. I have since I saw you stand up and talk at the old man's funeral, but I wouldn't touch you, because I had thought you were his lover." He held up his hand to hold off anything she might have said. "I now know that you weren't. I will say this again, I want you. I want to explore your body all night long. I want to be buried balls-deep inside you several times tonight. You can see how turned on I am about you. However, I won't do anything unless you tell me it's okay." Seth hadn't realized how much he wanted her to say yes until he stood there in all his naked glory, putting himself out there for her to decide whether she wanted to be with him or not.

"I know you're looking for an immediate answer, but I have an observation first."

"Which is?" Seth held his breath waiting for her reply.

"This, whatever we're going to do, does not interfere with our work. You can't go all he-man on me in a sticky situation."

Seth scowled at her, but he slowly nodded. "Whatever happens between us here in my home stays here. I will make sure it doesn't affect our work."

He sucked in his breath as a slow smile came over her face, and she moved the arm holding her towel, allowing it to drop as she held out her other arm toward him. "Well, I guess you better take me into the shower, then. It seems like I have missed some dirt from my own earlier."

"Fuck, yeah!" Seth yelled as he strode forward, and as the steam billowed out of the shower, he stepped between her legs, brought both hands up to her face, leaned in, and took her lips with his. It was the sweetest, hottest, most intense kiss he had ever remembered having before. If this kiss was any indication, then it would be fantastic to finally get inside her. Once he broke off the kiss for air, he stepped back to reach down and scoop her up. In no time he stepped into the shower, and set her on her feet, blocking the hot water as he quickly adjusted the temperature. With his back still taking the brunt of the water, he looked down at her and smiled, which was wiped off by the expression on her face. Before he could say anything, he felt his eyes widen as he watched her drop to her knees before him, and reach up to lightly cradle his engorged cock.

"Holy hell," Seth said through gritted teeth, then cried out when he felt and saw her hot mouth suck the tip of him inside. "Christ, Kora, you don't have to do that."

"I know." She pulled her mouth away from him long enough to answer, then put her hands on the back of his thighs to suck him into her mouth again. This time, she didn't stop until he felt himself hit the back of her throat, then he swore he went down further. It took everything Seth had in him not to explode in the back of her throat. To hold off the impending explosion, he reached down and squeezed the base of it. When she turned her scowl onto him, he gave her a sappy smile.

"If I don't pinch it off, I'm going to come. It's been a long time since someone has done that to me."

Kora smiled around his cock, and slowly moved her head back, making sure her teeth scraped along his length as she let him go. Once his cock was free from her mouth, she kissed the head, then slowly rose to her feet. Seth wasn't moving, and with a smile on her face, she grabbed the soap and began to lather her hands, then ran them over his wet skin. She had never seen anyone so toned, or sculpted before. She wanted every opportunity to run her hands freely over his gorgeous body. As she soaped her hands and ran them all over his chest, then around to his back, she smiled when she saw him close his eyes and swallow hard. From behind him, she reached around and ran her hands down his arms to his hands where he still held himself.

"Need some help there," she chuckled as she asked, then gave a little squeak when she found herself flat against the wall with Seth looming over her. The next thing she knew, he had her picked up and was staring in her face. With his jaw clenched, he asked, "Are you on any type of birth control?"

"I am, why? Where is the condom?"

"In my nightstand drawer. I won't make it to get one. I swear to you that I am clear. I got the results back at my last physical less than two months ago."

"I am too, I had them do the tests, not that I've been with a lot of men, but I wanted to make sure I was clear also."

"When did you get your results?"

"Last week, before I returned to work."

Seth closed his eyes, then lifted her higher, so her chest was even with his mouth, and with his eyes on hers, he clamped his mouth over one of her distended nipples, and watched the expressions flit across her face when he lightly bit down on her. "Put your hands on my shoulders," he ground out, and as soon as she did, he reached down to grab her ass and began to lift her higher. He only removed one hand to feel if she was ready for him, and when he brought his hand away wet, he looked her dead in the eye as he slowly entered her.

"Holy shit," Kora breathed out as she felt Seth's cock enter. She knew he was big, because she had seen him, and had even had him in her mouth, but it felt like he would tear her in two. She breathed in through her nose and out through her mouth when he slowed down to study her face. "I'm good, just go slow."

Seth nodded and continued, not stopping until he felt his balls touch her. With his head on the wall beside hers, he moved his mouth against her neck, and breathed in her scent.

"You feel so good," he said, and kissed her just below her ear. He smiled against her skin when she reached up and wrapped her arms around his neck and buried her hands in his wet hair.

"You feel good, too," she sighed, and brought his head over to hers so their lips could meet. They devoured one another until they had to come up for air, and as Kora used her inner muscles to massage Seth's cock inside her, his eyes flared as he looked down at her.

"Impatient?"

"Maybe," she said, but before she could say anything else, he backed all the way out, and when she went to tell him her displeasure, he slammed back in, causing her to call out.

"More!"

Seth took her for her word, and because she was held up by their hips locked together, he used his hands to come around, and wedged both thumbs between them. He ground out, "Look at me." She opened her eyes and then screamed when both his thumbs pinched her clit, and she flew over the edge of ecstasy, reaching in and biting his shoulder in the process of her orgasm. Seth continued to pound into her, and once he felt the tiny bite of pain, he returned the favor and as he spilled his seed into her, he grinned against her shoulder when she had another orgasm. He felt proud that he could get her off a second time. It was several minutes before they were able to get their breath back, and Seth wrapped his hands around Kora's bottom, gripped her ass cheeks, and stepped away from the wall. He turned them with the sole intention of allowing the water from the shower to cascade down Kora's back so she would feel better about standing on her feet. It didn't go as planned when she screamed bloody murder, then scrambled to get to the other side of the walk-in shower.

"What the fuck, Falco," she sputtered at him as she swung her wet hair out of her face, then reached for the door of the shower.

Confused, Seth stared at her and tried to take a step forward, but she held her hand out and at the last minute stepped back in and shoved him into the spray. He screamed, "What the fuck!" and tried to get away from the spray. The two of them ended up on the floor trying to scramble away from the icy blast coming from the shower head and ended up laughing too hard to get to their feet. Finally,

Seth walked on his knees to the controls and shut it off.

"Looks like you might need a new hot water tank."

"It's a fucking forty-gallon tank," Seth scowled, then looked at her with a stink eye. "How long was your shower before I met you in the hall?"

Kora opened her mouth to deny she was the one to cause them to run out of hot water, but quickly closed it. "Oops," she giggled, and took the hand Seth offered her to help her off the floor. "Sorry."

Seth looked at her sternly, then smirked when he saw her naked body before him. "Well, at least we were able to get the dirt off ourselves." He laughed when Kora looked down at her chest, to the spot he had run his finger over earlier and left a trail of dirt in its wake. With a grin they went out into his bedroom, and before she could take two steps, he tossed her one of his tees from the pile on the end of his bed.

"At least it's the same color," Kora said as she slipped it over her wet body and grabbed one of her towels from earlier and began to dry her hair.

"What do you mean by that?"

"It means that yes, this is your firefighter tee, and it has Fool's Gold FD on the back, but if you recall, the lettering is yellow, not white."

Seth looked at her with a frown then his face cleared. "I never thought of that. Me being a captain, and you a lieutenant, our lettering is yellow, the others are white."

"Correct, and Troy has to wear a white button down, since he is the chief."

"That I don't envy him at all."

"Do you envy him because he is the chief?" Kora asked as she stood there and watched him dress, not ashamed to be caught admiring his body as he did so.

"Nope." By his statement she could tell he was serious. He took it one step further, and once he was dressed, he turned to her fully and nodded once. "I was a MOS7051 for over twenty years, and by the end of my career, I was a Commander of the unit. I don't envy Troy one bit for being the chief and having to make all the decisions about budgets, personnel, payroll, and all that shit."

From his expression, Kora believed him, and nodded. "Just one question," she asked as they exited Seth's bedroom, and she paused outside the room she had taken for herself.

"What's that?" Seth scowled at her, then opened the door they stood before, walked in, picked up her bag, then walked back out and went to his room, where he tossed her go bag on the bed. When he rejoined her, he grinned. "You'll be sleeping with me, what we had in the shower was nowhere near enough time. I want you again already, but I think we need food first. What was your question?"

Kora looked at him in shock, then grinned as she looked down and saw his shirt came to the middle of her thighs and she didn't feel her ass hanging out, so she shrugged and went with it. "What is MOS7051?"

Seth led the way down to the kitchen, and said over his shoulder, "Marie Corps Firefighter. I became a firefighter for the Corps two weeks into my basic training."

"Really?" Kora asked in shock as she followed him downstairs, and they both gravitated to the kitchen. She stopped suddenly to look around wildly.

"What's wrong?"

"Will your brothers and their girlfriends come barging in here like they did this morning?"

"Naw, they only invade my space in the mornings," Seth chuckled as he looked at her, then went over and placed his hands on her hips as he further explained. "I don't know if you realized this, but I'm not a very talkative person. It's not that I don't like my family, it's just that I don't know them. I've spent more time away from them than with them. They know I don't like them to crowd me on a regular basis, so they decided to invade my house in the morning, as Troy likes to tell me, it's so they know I'm up and about."

"Is there a reason why you wouldn't be, up and about, that is?"

"Nope, it's just their way of letting me know they're in my life."

Neither spoke after that and together they began making a meal, and while Seth went out to start the grill for the steaks he'd gotten out of the freezer earlier, Kora stayed in the kitchen to prepare the potatoes, and a salad. When she was done with her part, she went out on the back porch and looked around.

"I didn't really pay attention earlier while I was weeding your flower beds, but what are those buildings?" She pointed in the direction she had seen lights way off in the distance.

"That's where the guys live." Seth came up and wrapped an arm around her shoulders to bring her closer, then used the hand holding the BBQ fork to point. "That's the bunkhouse, it's where Heath and Tessa live. The next building is the old stable, and Troy and Esme live there. Then there is the barn, where Trent lives, and lastly is Marcus and Charli's house. There used to be an old equipment shed there, and Marcus parks his helicopter in the field behind it, but it was blown up a couple of months ago, and Charli rebuilt there. Don't worry," he chuckled at her expression as he turned back to the grill to flip the steaks. "They all converted their individual building into living space, it's not as bad as it sounds. We'll have to go over there after we get off from work next time, it's too late tonight."

"Okay," Kora said, and couldn't begin to picture what he had been talking about. In no time Seth had the steaks on a platter and they went inside to eat their dinner.

CHAPTER 10

"Penny for your thoughts," Seth said as he sat back from finishing his meal and pushed his plate away. He really wanted a beer, but he had to be on duty the next day and he didn't drink when he had to go to work. The only time he had anything strong to drink was when he was off for seventy-two hours straight. He knew he could have one, but it was just his way of making sure that he wouldn't be impaired in any way to do his job. When he studied Kora, he frowned when her previously open expression shut down.

"Stop," Seth said, then leaned forward and took one of her hands in his. "We're going to be in each other's pockets for God knows how long, not only do we work together, but we are living together until we can confirm if it's Trumbull that's after you, and we can take him down. On top of that, we're having sex, so don't shut down when I ask you what you are thinking. I want you to be honest with me whenever you have something to say. Without that, none of this will work."

Seth sat there with her hand in his and watched her face. It took everything he had not to laugh at the different expressions going across it. He really liked how her nose wrinkled as she acted like something was bad.

"Fine," Kora sighed, and took her hand away from his. She couldn't talk while she was doing skin on skin contact with him, it was too distracting. "I was sitting here picturing how your kitchen could be different. Not that I have any say in the matter, and not to dismiss your home, but it needs to be updated. I swear it was built in the forties or fifties and they are calling to take it back."

Seth threw his head back and laughed, causing Kora to suck in her breath at his handsomeness. He had to use his napkin to wipe his eyes. "It is ugly, isn't it. So far, since moving in here, I've only had Charli put the bathroom in off my bedroom. Eventually I want to upgrade the entire house, but I figured I'd wait until I was in a better routine. I don't know whether you know this or not, but Heath was injured in a fire last month, and is still on restrictive duty. Though he doesn't work directly out of our house, he still helps out and we had to shuffle people around and we put him on the ladder truck to man the controls until he's better."

"How bad?"

"Not that bad, he dislocated his knee. As long as he follows the doctor's orders and continues with his PT, he'll be fine. He's almost healed, but we don't want to push our luck. I'm not saying this to get you upset, but you weren't the only one out after the fire that took out Chief Jade. Though you are the only one that came back. Between you and me, and we'll have to talk to Troy about it this next week, but I don't think the others will be back. We're short-handed, and as long at Heath can man the controls for the ladder truck, we're better now that you're back, but we're still not out of the woods yet."

"How many guys are out?"

"Only three now that you're back."

"Oh wow, I did not know anyone else was injured."

"Yeah, the bitch of it was that two of them didn't know it until a few days later. They thought they'd only gotten scuffed up, but it turned out to be more serious than that."

"How bad?"

"One had cracked ribs, but during the next fire they broke, so he's still out. The other thought he had twisted his ankle and knee when that beam fell on you, but that wasn't the case."

"Hairline fracture?"

"Yes, in the ankle, but torn ligaments in the knee."

"Ouch."

"Yeah, we're grateful that you are back, and Troy has been making noises of looking through the applications from the academy, but it will be some time, because the new class for candidates doesn't start for another two weeks."

"Shit." Kora sighed.

"Yes, but we're making do. Now tell me, what were you thinking about earlier when I asked for your thoughts?"

Kora shrugged, then looked him directly in the eye. "I was redesigning your kitchen in my head. As I said a few minutes ago, this kitchen was probably great back in the day, but nowadays it won't cut it. Who in their right mind would have orange Formica countertops with yellow and brown backsplash and linoleum floors the same color?"

"I know," Seth chuckled. "It takes some getting used to, but like I said, I'd like to wait until I know exactly what I want before I talk with Charli." Seth looked around at his kitchen and saw it once again through someone else's eyes. After several minutes, he looked at Kora and asked, "What would *you* do to change it?"

"It's not my house."

"I didn't say it was, or wasn't, but come on,

Kora, I'm a guy, the décor doesn't really bother me. I was in the military for twenty years, drab olive green and sand brown are the colors I'm used to." He shrugged and saw her wrinkle her nose. It took everything he had not to pull her into his lap, kiss the wrinkle away, and hug her as they discussed how she would redesign his kitchen. When she still didn't say anything, he sighed and asked, "Okay, let me ask you this, would you tear down any walls to do what they call the open concept thing? There have been many conversations along those lines with my siblings."

"No." Kora's response was quick, and then she stated why. Seth leaned back and listened to everything she had to say, not interrupting her, liking her ideas. As she talked, he grabbed a pad of paper from behind him and began writing what she said down.

"First, I'd get rid of the floor, countertops, and back splash. I like the vintage look of the cupboards, but that's me. It's your house, so you'd have to decide what to do with them."

"What would you do?"

"Take them down and power wash them. Give them a good scrubbing, and maybe paint them a light sage green." She looked at him with a grin. "Green is my favorite color. Then I'd do the same with the bottom cabinets. Scrub the hell out of them and paint them two shades darker than the upper ones. I would leave the sink as is, again scrubbing it. When I was out on disability, I watched those home improvement shows and everyone wanted what they called a farmer's sink, and you have one already, which is original to the house. I'd keep it."

"What would you do with the appliances?"

Kora looked at him, rolled her eyes, and then laughed. "Replace them."

"No shit, but with what?"

"New ones."

"Alright smartass, would you do stainless steel?"

"No, I would do what they call black stainless steel. It's a different color." She reached for her phone she'd set on the table when she'd come in from weeding the flowerbed, and accessed the internet. Once she found what she wanted, she went to stand next to him, but Seth guided her to sit on his leg as she pointed to what she'd found. "See, they're not quite the color of stainless steel, but they aren't black either. Lighter than one, darker than the other. But that's what I would do in here, and the countertops I would do granite." Her fingers flew over the keys on her phone, and she looked at him with a smile. "This is what I would do them in. It's not completely green, and it's not completely white. With the cabinets being green, you'd need some brightness in here. Then I'd do some track lighting, and if possible, make the window bigger, letting in more light."

"Would you put an island in?"

"No, it would take away from the originality of the place. Fifty, sixty years ago, they didn't have islands in their kitchens. I'd save the space for a larger kitchen table. Since your brothers join you for breakfast already, and I'm sure you'll end up with a wife someday, and Trent will eventually find someone, you'd want a table big enough for all of you, and something you can add leaves to when your family grows." She didn't look at him as she said this, but Seth could picture what she'd described, and it did not bother him that he pictured her sitting at the table with their children. He cleared his throat, and nodded.

"I like your ideas, I'll have to do some research, and I might talk with Charli about them soon."

"Hey, don't let me guide you, if you're going to do anything, wait until you find a permanent girl-friend or wife. My ideas might be totally different from theirs."

"I like your ideas," Seth said, and hugged her to him. "I've been trying to wrack my brain around how to keep the kitchen as is, but updating it, you know. Charli keeps telling me I need to knock out walls and open it up to other parts of the house. I personally like the individual rooms, that's why I picked living in the house, and the others picked where they live now. Would you keep the hardware on the cupboards?"

"Yes, it's what they would consider antique now, but I'd do the same as with the cupboards, I'd pressure wash them because of all the years of grime on them. Not to say the previous owners didn't clean them, but you understand what I'm saying, right?"

"I do," Seth said as he nodded, and pushed his notes away. He wrapped his other arm around her and kissed her neck. "Thank you for bringing a new kitchen to my mind. It's not like I don't trust Charli, she is a contractor after all and she put in my new bath, but I want to keep as much of the house original as I can. I know this sounds crazy, but the first time I walked in here I had this overwhelming sense of home come over me, and I want to keep that, but make it mine too."

"I totally understand. This house has a good vibe about it, it does feel like home, and it's screaming to have a family living here. I can picture kids coming down the stairs on Christmas morning and seeing all the presents under the tree." She sighed and didn't see Seth's reaction as he pictured the same thing. Not wanting to get ahead of himself, because again, he pictured Kora as the mother of those children, he hugged her to him, and they sat like that for a long time before breaking apart. Neither said a word as they rose together and silently cleaned up the kitchen from their supper. When they were done, Seth stood with his hips leaned against the counter and studied her.

"What?"

"I don't want to assume anything here, but I have a question for you. I'm only asking, because I've never had anything over a one-night stand before."

"What are you asking?" Kora asked, and held her breath for his reply.

"Will you spend the night in my bed with me? I'm not being crass, but if we have sex, then we have sex. If we don't, we don't. I don't want to put any pressure on you, but I would like to have you in my bed."

Kora shrugged as she looked him dead in the eye. "Okay, but I have to warn you, I'm going to be getting up a few minutes early so I can swing by my place on the way to work. I want to feed the cats and gather today's mail."

"How long will it take?"

"Ten minutes, fifteen tops. Do you think I can leave here fifteen minutes before you and stop in to do that, then I'll meet you at the station."

Seth drew in a deep breath and let it out slowly. "I don't see why not, from what I understand of Trumbull so far, he's not one to go out of his way for anything. I don't see what difference fifteen minutes would make." He walked toward her and gathered her in his arms, and for the first time in over thirty years he felt like he was coming home when she wrapped her arms around his waist, and laid her head on his chest. He laid his cheek on the top of her head and breathed her in. They stayed like that for several minutes before they broke apart. While Kora made sure the coffee pot was ready for the next morning, with the timer programed, Seth made sure the back door was locked.

Kora frowned at him as he held out his hand to her, and together, they made their way up the stairs. "If you lock the door, how do the guys get in here in the morning?"

"The sons of a bitches have their own key," Seth laughed at his own confession. "Troy was the one to get them all made. We all have keys to the others' places, in case of emergency." He laughed again. "But I did give a key to Charli when she was building my bathroom. Who knows how the others got a copy, as long as they don't come in all hours of the night, I'm okay with it as it stands. Fortunately, they only come over for breakfast."

"You really like them, don't you?"

"I do, I just feel so bad that I wasn't there when they were growing up. I bought the Paradise Ranch and offered them to come here to live just before Jake and Hank asked us to come work for the

Fool's Gold Fire Department. They asked right around the time of the old man's funeral."

"May I ask why you purchased the ranch?"

"Well, I didn't purchase it by myself. I was going to, but the boys convinced me that if we were all going to live here, then they wanted to pay for their part. I did it as a good faith effort to reach out to them to let them know that I wanted us to be a family."

They continued up the stairs and into Seth's bedroom, neither of them talking as they got ready for bed. Since Kora already wore Seth's shirt, she left it on, and brushed her teeth before crawling beneath the covers. They continued their conversation as they settled in the bed, with Kora on her back, and Seth on his side with his head propped on his hand, and his other hand on her stomach.

"Weren't you a family already?" Kora asked, to prompt him to continue. What he was telling her didn't sound like anything that she knew of their father, but she couldn't tell him he was wrong, because she had only been with Shawn four days a year, not with him twenty-four seven.

"Yes and no. See, I was seventeen when I left for the Marines. The twins were fourteen, and Marcus was only four. I never even found out about Heath until years later. He came around after I left, he was sixteen when he showed up."

"He's younger than you, but older than the twins?"

"Yes, proving the old man had an extramarital affair. It took me a long time to realize this, but I now think he was so hard on me when Mom and Grandpa died in that fire because he was at Heath's place spending time with him and his mother. It was *his* guilt that he projected onto me, and he never got over it, not if his treatment of me was any indication. That's why I left at the age of seventeen. I know you hold him in high regard, but I just can't. I'm sorry."

"No, I understand. I realize now that I only spent time with him four days a year. I also know that he distracted me those days, and made sure I was okay. Other than that, I never saw him, not until I was around twenty-two and began working at his fire station. I only worked with him for a couple of years before I transferred to Fool's Gold. Before you ask, we worked at the same station, but not on the same shift. Again, I didn't see him all the time. I'm not going to get on your bandwagon and start hating him like you do, but I won't shove the good qualities I know of him down your throat."

"Thank you for that. Let's just agree to disagree on our feelings about Shawn Falco. I can live with that, and I'll take a page from your book and not shove his bad behavior down your throat."

"Agreed." She nodded and reached up to kiss his

cheek. They settled down in the bed, and for the first time that Seth could ever remember, he wrapped his arms around a woman and settled in for the night. He couldn't even remember when he fell asleep with her in his arms. All he knew was that he had the best night of sleep he'd had in a long time.

CHAPTER 11

Kora pulled into her usual parking spot at her apartment building, and hurried over to the front entrance. Using her key, she let herself in, then she hustled over to her mailbox to gather her mail. She had forgotten to grab it when Seth had come home with her two days ago after their long shift so she could pack a bag to go to his place because of the person that was after her. With her hands full, knowing the elevator took forever, she ran up the five flights to her apartment. She let herself in, went through it quickly to see if anything was out of place, then satisfied all was well, she went to the kitchen and grabbed a plastic baggie and filled it with the cat food she kept in a lower cupboard. In less than five minutes she was out the door, making sure she grabbed several magazines that had been in her mail. She would read them between calls at the station to keep from getting bored out of her mind. She made a mental note to go to the library to pick up the next book in the series she was reading, but knew she couldn't do anything for the next twenty-four hours, since she would be on duty then.

Kora jogged back down the stairs, and instead of going out of the front door, she went to the back of the building, and let herself out the door the tenants used to take their garbage out of. She made sure she had her keys, and then secured the door behind her. With the baggie of food in her hand, she started toward the dumpster where she had left the cat dishes. Seeing them empty, she dumped the food in it, and looked up with a grin. Standing there staring at her was the most adorable cat she had ever seen. She didn't know what kind it was, but it was the type that had a smushed up face, and its ears were close to its head. Not knowing if the gray and white cat was male or female, she held out her hand and wiggled her fingers. The cat looked down it's smushed up nose at her, and looked through her. Kora chuckled as she looked at the cat, shook her head, and stood. The next thing she knew, her head bounced off the side of the metal dumpster, and instinctively, she kicked out, and heard a grunt. The next thing she knew, she was being hit in the head, and as she kicked out, her attacker grunted again when she made contact with their knee, and they stumbled.

Kora saw was the glint of what she assumed was a knife and when she tried to back away, her attacker lunged as he swung his arm out toward her. She didn't feel the burning pain in her side right away, but swore. "Son of a bitch." Again, she went on the attack and this time she held up her arms like a fighter and egged him on. "Come on you fucker, let's see what you have." When the man limped toward her, she dropped to her hands and swung one foot out, connecting with his knee. This time he went down, but before Kora could do anything, she saw a blur, and heard a deep growl, along with the scream of a cat. Suddenly there was a gigantic cat attacking her attacker around the head and face. The cat sounded like it was being murdered, while the man was screaming and trying to get the cat off his face. Kora took the opportunity to come up behind the man and kick him in the knee she's already damaged twice in as many minutes, and because she wanted proof of who her attacker was, because he was wearing a ski mask, she reached up to the back of his head and tore it off, making sure she pulled his hair in the process. If she didn't recognize him, then she knew she could give the cap to the police, and they could run it for DNA. She wasn't completely stupid.

Suddenly the man let out a scream to rival the

cat's, then the cat went flying through the air. Before Kora could move, he whipped around, and punched her in the face, then screamed at her. "You're a dead woman, you fucking bitch!" Then, he hobbled away. Kora's vision had gone blurry from the punch, and the next thing she knew her friend Sparrow Oakley was squatted beside her with a hand on her shoulder, talking to her.

"Huh? What?"

"Kora, what happened? Your neighbors called in a disturbance coming from this back alley. I heard the commotion in the background noise from the call and rushed right over. Can you tell me what happened?" The deputy sheriff watched at Kora's eyes rolled to the back of her head, and as she swore, she gently laid Kora out on her back, then swore harder when she saw the wetness on the side of Kora's dark blue tee. She frowned as she lifted it, then swore at the large gash with the blood pouring out. Sparrow immediately used the mic on her shoulder to call for the ambulance.

"WHERE'S KORA?" Heath asked Seth the next morning as they both climbed out of their trucks at the fire station. He hadn't been at Seth's house that morning for breakfast, and no one questioned his absence.

"She had to swing by her apartment to gather her mail and feed some stray cats in the alley behind her house. She should be here any minute."

"Oh," Heath said as he started toward the station.

"How's the knee? I noticed you limped a little."

"I'm good, it only acts up after I've been sitting for a while. The more I walk, the better it is. Doctor said I should be back to full duty in a week."

Together they walked toward the fire station carrying their turn-out gear, along with their go bag for their shift. They took care of their gear, and headed toward the kitchen, where Troy would have roll call and they would talk with the leaving shift. They were joined by others, and they all stopped and cocked their head to the side when the alarm sounded, and there was a call for the ambulance. Because they were a small fire station, the trucks went out with every call, whether they were needed or not. They went, because you never knew whether some muscle was needed on an ambulance call or not.

Seth turned on his heel and jogged to the truck he'd just put his turn-out gear in, and as he settled in, he removed his shoes, and stuffed his feet into his boots. In seconds he had his gear on, and looked over at Eric as he climbed in, did the same and in less than three minutes from the alarm sounding, they were out the door and heading to the address of the call. Eric parked on the street, leaving room for the ambulance to pull closer to the entrance to the alley.

As Seth jumped down from the fire truck, he was joined by his brothers, and Troy led the way. They didn't have long to go before they were met by Sparrow Oakley. Not only was she a friend of theirs, but she was also the Lieutenant Sheriff of the county stationed here out of Fool's Gold.

"What's up?" Troy asked as he was joined by the other firemen.

"It's not good, Chief. It's one of your own."

"Excuse me?"

"We got a call into the station that it sounded like a cat was being murdered. I heard it in the background noise from the call. I rushed over, and when I arrived, I found the victim sitting on the ground, but they were weaving back and forth, like they were hurt. As I was talking, they passed out and on a quick initial exam I found a knife wound to the abdomen, that's why I called it in."

"Okay," Seth said as he looked down the alleyway and couldn't see the victim because the ambulance crew was working on her.

"It's Kora," Sparrow said and had to jump back when the oldest Falco brother lunged for her, and his brothers held him back.

"What did you say?"

"It's Kora, Kora Garrison, and by the looks of it

she was attacked. I'll have to wait until she comes to in order to get her statement." She was talking to the empty space in front of her, because Seth had broken out in a dead run to get down the alley, with his brothers hot on his heels.

"Son of a bitch," Seth said as he dropped to his knees at Kora's head, and laid one hand on the side of her face. As he studied that beautiful face, the face he had kissed every inch of just that morning, the area around one eye spreading both toward her nose and her ear began to form a dark bruise.

"We have to go, One," the EMT driver said, and it took Marcus and Trent to lift Seth from the ground to move him, so the EMTs could do their job. Seth looked around wildly, and Troy grabbed his bicep and nodded. "Go, we got this. Call us when you hear something."

That was all the encouragement Seth needed. "I'm going with you," he said as he helped lift the stretcher, and put Kora's prone body on the gurney and they ran to the ambulance.

"I'll meet you at the hospital!" Sparrow yelled after them, and Seth only raised a hand in acknowledgement before he climbed into the back, and sat to one side as Brad worked on Kora.

"How bad is it?" Seth asked through gritted teeth.

"I have no clue why she passed out, my guess is she has a concussion, and based on the bruise forming on her face, I'd say her attacker hit her. She's going to need stitches, but the cut isn't deep."

"What cut?" Seth asked, and stared in shock when Brad lifted Kora's shirt and showed him the three-inch gash on her side. He winced at all the blood coming out, but from his experience he knew it looked worse than it was. He looked around, and because he knew the inside of the ambulance, he began opening drawers, and when he found what he wanted, he pulled out three of the same items. He donned a pair of gloves and nodded at Brad's scowl.

"If she was attacked, then she might have the guy's DNA on her," he said as with his gloved hands, he removed the ski mask still clasped tightly in her hand into a plastic bag, then took the other two bags and put them over her hands. "Maybe she scratched him or something, but I'd bet my next paycheck that she ripped that mask off his head."

"Good thinking. I was about to rip it out of her hand and toss it away, so I'm glad I didn't," Brad said, then scowled. "Hey, wasn't she attacked out on that grass fire last weekend?"

"She was, and this is all my fault. I was supposed to be protecting her, but she wanted to stop by her place on the way into work to get her mail and feed some alley cats. We parted ways only five minutes before the alarm went off. I swear it was only five minutes, but if she was attacked, it had to have been longer."

"He might have been waiting for her, you know. If he's a stalker, maybe he knew her schedule and lay in wait." Brad shrugged, like it was no big deal.

Seth was seething inside. Kora being hurt was his fault. If he had gone with her, none of this would have happened. He shouldn't have allowed her to go by herself. As soon as they pulled into the hospital, he jumped out first, and watched as Brad and the driver, whose name escaped Seth at this time, rushed the gurney out and into the emergency entrance. He called out that he would be right there. As soon as they entered the door, he walked several feet away, and pulled his phone. When Jake Cogburn answered, he didn't mince his words as he spoke.

"It's Seth Falco, I fucked up. It's all my fault."

"What happened?"

"Kora was attacked and I wasn't there. I allowed her to stop by her apartment to feed her cat and gather her mail on her way into work this morning. The call came in at three minutes after seven, I left her at five minutes to seven. I understand if you want to take me off her protection duty, and assign someone else to her."

"Where are you?"

"The hospital."

"I'm on my way," Jake said, and before Seth

could say anything, Jake hung up on him. In less than ten minutes, Jake was there, right along with Sparrow. Seth was still outside. He told himself that he was waiting for Jake, but in reality, he didn't, or couldn't handle the fact that Kora had been hurt on his watch.

As soon as he was joined by Jake and Sparrow, he held out the plastic bag and shoved it in Sparrow's direction. "Here."

"What's this?" At first Sparrow wouldn't take it, but as soon as Seth began talking, she grabbed the bag and nodded.

"Kora had this grasped in her hand. I believe her attacker may have been wearing this and she ripped it off their head. I don't know if you can get DNA from where he breathed on it, maybe some spit or something, hell, she might even have pulled his hair in the process of ripping it off. I also took the liberty of covering her hands with more plastic bags to preserve any evidence she might have been able to get. I don't know how close she was able to get to him."

"I left my deputies knocking on doors, and checking to see if there is any film in the cameras we saw. There aren't any in the alley, but there are some on businesses at each end. We'll see if we can't get a description of the attacker, or a vehicle, or even a plate. We'll find who did this."

"Look into a guy by the name of Darryl Trumbull," Seth said, and turned to Jake. "I understand if you want to take me off the case."

"Christ, Cogburn, this is one of yours?" Sparrow looked at him in shock.

"It is, and no, Falco, you're staying on the case. I hadn't gotten back to you, but with the information you called into me I was able to do some digging." Jake turned to Sparrow and gave a heavy sigh. "We need to talk. Our suspect is as Seth said, Darryl Trumbull."

"Who is he?" Sparrow asked as she pulled her little notebook from her breast pocket, clicked her pen, ready to take notes.

"He's a firefighter from Colorado Springs that was hurt in the arson fire that covered up Chief Jade's murder."

"Okay, but if he's from Colorado Springs, what's he doing going after one of our own over there in Fool's Gold?"

"Apparently, he's got it into his head that all his problems within the fire department are Kora's fault. I did some digging and they, Trumbull and Kora went through the fire academy together. Kora beat him out in everything, she excelled in all the classes and tests, while he was middle ground to mediocre at best. Kora went to Denver after the academy, and Trumbull went to Colorado Springs."

"So why is he after her now? I'm assuming it's been a while since their paths have crossed."

"It has. Again, I did a lot of digging in the last twenty-four hours, and it turns out that along with being a tool, Trumbull didn't pass his psych evaluation to return to work after the fire. Here's a copy of what I've got so far. You're more than welcome to it, and if you don't mind, I'll continue to look into him."

"Not at all. I've learned from experience to take all the help from the Brotherhood Protection Agency that I can. You know we're still short-staffed and don't have the manpower, let alone the man hours to do as much digging as you do. Just remember, if there's something you can't find out, or need help looking into, let me know, and I can take it from there."

"Thanks, Sparrow, but I think you'll find a plethora of information that I've gathered so far. It seems that Trumbull took the exam to become a lieutenant several times, and failed each time. In the course of my research, I believe he was taking the exam for the second time when Kora took hers. She passed with flying colors, he did not. I think that started his hatred for her. I'm only guessing here, but it's like he had to blame someone beside himself on his failures, and he had a past with Kora from the academy..." Jake let his statement trail off, and Seth nodded.

"I can see it. If he was mediocre at best in his time at the academy, and after what Esme told us about him, though I don't know him, I can see someone like that blaming someone else, someone he feels wronged him in any way. Always someone else's fault, never his own."

"Also," Sparrow waited to continue until they both looked at her. "I'll try to see if I can see anything in his background that would tell me how he feels about women in authority. It sounds like he's jealous of a woman besting him. Do you know if there are women superiors over at the Colorado Springs firehouse?"

"I'm not sure," Jake said at the same time Seth answered. "There are three of them."

"Ah, thanks, Falco. This is something to look into. Thanks for giving me the heads-up, Jake. Now I have to get in there and see if I can get a statement from Kora."

"One thing I can tell you about her attacker," Seth said as he turned on the heel of his fire boot to walk beside Sparrow as they entered the emergency room. Jake walked on her other side.

"What's that?"

"The fucker, whoever it was, hit her. As she lay there on the ground, then in the ambulance, I watched her beautiful face forming a bruise from her nose to her ear."

"Fucker," Sparrow whispered beneath her breath, and neither one of them saw the grin from Jake at Seth's description of Kora's looks.

CHAPTER 12

Seth stood with Sparrow and Jake as the nurse looked up and nodded to Sparrow. "You're here for Kora Garrison?"

"I am, how is she?"

"She's getting stitched up. The doctor should be out shortly, but she is awake."

Seth hadn't realized he'd been holding his breath, until Jake grabbed his arm to keep his from falling when he heard that Kora was awake.

"Do you know if she has a concussion?" he asked, and when the nurse gave him the stink eye, Sparrow was the one to speak.

"He's not only her co-worker, but he's her protector from the Brotherhood."

"Ah, we don't know that yet, they're still running tests. I'm sure once she's stitched up you can go back to see her." They all nodded and stood off to one side as they waited for the doctor. It seemed like hours to Seth, but according to the clock he had been staring at it was only thirty-five minutes before they were told they could go back. Seth was the first one in the curtained area, and he stopped so suddenly, that Sparrow ran into the back of him. Jake had to reach out to catch her, and he shoved Seth forward so they could get into the room

"Holy shit, kid," Jake said to Kora as he caught sight of her. "It looks like you went fifteen rounds with Ali."

"Thanks, it feels like it, but I went one round with a dumpster, the second round was with a fist."

"God, I'm so sorry, this is all my fault," Seth said as he walked up to her head, then leaned down and kissed the bruise on the side of her head. He had thought she had only one black eye, but it was worse because she had two.

"It's not your fault. Whether you had been there or not, he still would have attacked me." She looked around wildly, then scowled. "I could have sworn I had his ski mask in my hand when he punched me in the face."

"You did," Seth said. "I took it from you in the ambulance, and I bagged your hands, hoping you had gotten some DNA off him."

"I don't know about that, but I made sure to pull his hair when I pulled the mask off his face."

"I'll look into it," Sparrow said as she held up the plastic bag Seth had given her when she'd first arrived. "What can you tell me about the attack."

"Not much. When I got home, I parked in my usual spot, used my key to let myself in the front door, gathered my mail, jogged up to my apartment." She looked at them with a grin, then winced when it pulled on her split lip. "It was faster than the elevator. I tossed my mail on the counter, walked around, and found nothing out of place, then grabbed a baggie and filled it with cat food."

"Why would you have to check to see if anything was out of place at your place?" Sparrow asked with a frown.

"I stayed with Seth since being off shift. Oh, shit." She looked at Jake and Seth, then back at Jake. "You didn't tell her?"

"About?" Jake scowled at her, then shook his head in confusion. "I don't know what you're asking."

"You didn't tell Sparrow that someone took a shot at me while we were out at that grass fire four days ago?"

"Someone fucking shot you?" Sparrow demanded and turned her wrath onto Jake. "I get what the Brotherhood does, and I appreciate you keeping me informed on your cases, and even helping with the research, but I need to be informed of things like bullets flying around my county."

"I know, and I'm sorry. Hank said he would stop by and inform you when he went out of town."

"Patterson was here?"

"Yes, that's when we told Seth that he should be the one to protect Kora. They work together, so he wouldn't have to be a nuisance at her job. He's there already, and living out on the Paradise Ranch, it's so remote that no one would find her there. I'm not sure what, if any, protection was put up after Bart blew up Marcus' helicopter, but it was the safest place for her to be. I'm sorry Hank didn't inform you about someone taking a shot at Kora."

"I want a report."

"I'll have it to you before the end of the day," Jake said sheepishly.

"See that you do," Sparrow said, then turned back to Kora. "You made sure your place was undisturbed?" she asked, picking up the conversation again.

"Yes, then I gathered the cat food and took it down to the alley. I accessed the alley using the back door that the tenants use to take our garbage out to the dumpster. I gathered the food dish, made sure it was cleaned out, then saw one of the cats. I tried to get it, I don't know whether it is a he or she, because they won't let me get close to them, but I tried to get it to come to me. It is a beautiful gray and white cat, the type that has the smushed face and small ears.

Seth's heart did a jerk in the center of his chest when she wrinkled her nose to mimic how the cat should look. He smirked at Jake when he barked out a laugh at her description.

"The next thing I know, my head was slammed against the dumpster. I don't know whether he used his hand or not. All I know is that I was able to regain my balance quickly and I kicked out. I made contact with his knee, I believe it was his knee. We fought, he pulled a knife, and when I tried to get away, he lunged at me. I didn't realize he'd cut me until after everything was done."

"What happened next?" Sparrow had been taking notes, and she only exchanged a small smile with Jake when they both watched as Seth reached down and took Kora's hand in his, encouraging her to continue with her story.

"I don't really know, it's all a blur. After he cut me, I kicked his knee again, then all of a sudden, he's screaming bloody murder, and I hear a cat screaming like it's being killed. I kicked his knee again, from behind, and that's when I ripped the ski mask off him. The next thing I know, that gray cat goes flying through the air, and this guy, before you ask, I swear I've never seen him before in my life, but he whips around, tells me I'm a dead bitch, then punches me. It happened so fast, the next thing I know I'm waking up here in the hospital."

"I was on scene," Sparrow said. "I was talking to you, but you weren't responding. Then your eyes rolled to the back of your head, and you passed out. I called it in."

"What time did the call come in?" Kora asked Seth.

"Seven oh three," Seth answered.

"He must have been waiting for me. I was in and out of my apartment in under two minutes, three tops." She sighed as she leaned back on the bed, and everyone looked up when the curtain was pulled back and a doctor walked in. No one said a word until Kora spoke.

"Well? Can I go to work?"

"No, but you can be released."

"What do you mean no?" Both Seth and Kora demanded as one. "Are the stitches that bad?" Seth asked.

"The stitches are fine, as long as she keeps them covered while at work, she could work, but she can't work for the next thirty-six hours because she has a mild concussion." The doctor looked at her with a frown. "Do you have someone to keep an eye on you?"

"Yes, but I'm going to have to do it at the

station," Kora said, then glared when the doctor started to talk. "Give me a note for my boss, and I'll not work for thirty-six hours, but you can bet your ass I'll be back to work in seventy-two." She looked at Seth and they exchanged smiles, then looked at the confusion on the doctor's face.

"It's our work schedule. I'm on for the next twenty-four, then off for forty-eight, then on for seventy-two."

"Whatever, I want you off for the next thirty-six. Have someone with you at all times, and if you feel dizzy, or pass out, come back here."

"Thanks, Doc. Can I take something for this headache?"

"I'd stick it out as long as you can, but if it's too bad take Tylenol. If that doesn't help, come back here."

"Okay," Kora said, and swung her legs over the side of the bed, and sat there until the room stopped spinning. She looked at Seth when he went to say something, but her look had him holding his tongue. He couldn't resist when she wrinkled her nose at him, so he bent down and quickly kissed it.

"I'll drive you back to the station."

"I said no work," the doctor said from behind him. The tone of his voice sounded like he was yelling at them, which he probably was, but Seth's tone of voice caused him to look away from him.

"I'm her person, and I have to report to work. She will be at the station with me, so I and the other firefighters and EMTs can keep an eye on her."

"Oh," was his only answer, then he turned on his heel and left. Before Kora got off the bed, she looked at Sparrow. "Do you have any more questions?"

"Not at this time, but if you think of anything, write it down. You have my number, so call me if you do remember anything."

"I will, Sparrow. Thanks for being there for me."

"It's my job to be there for the citizens of Fool's Gold, I'm just glad you're going to be okay."

"Yeah, but I just got back to work. I don't want to be out again."

Sparrow leaned in like she was imparting a big secret and she whispered loudly. "Have Falco here stop at the farmers' market on the way back to the station."

"Shit, I don't have my truck here." Seth looked at them in shock.

"I'll take you back," Jake said. "Why would they want to go to the farmers' market?"

"Because I know Kora, when she's upset, or pissed, she cooks. The farmers' market has a new shipment of apples that just came in fresh from the orchard."

"Hot damn," Kora said, then whipped her head around to talk to Seth, but she had to grab his hand when the room spun. "I'm okay, but do you think we can stop? I can make apple pies for the station."

"Let's go," Seth grinned. "Apple pie is my favorite." They finished up the discharge papers, and Jake gave them a ride to the farmers' market, Kora told Seth what she wanted, and in no time, he had gotten the items, and they were on their way back to the station. They arrived back there by eight thirty, and Kora had to report to Troy that she was unable to work, though she would still be at the station. Because she was under Seth's protection, he agreed with it and let her go, but not before informing her that she wasn't allowed to even do her paperwork.

Disappointed, Kora made her way to the kitchen and after accessing the supplies, she washed her hands, pushed up her sleeves, and got to work. Hours later, the members of the firehouse sat down to a meal of stuffed peppers, salad, home-made garlic bread, and for dessert, they had a choice of a slice of apple pie, or a serving of apple crisp. Kora grinned when the Falco brothers opted for a little of both. It surprised her when all the men told her to go rest in the common area while they cleaned up the kitchen. They had all just sat down to enjoy their evening when the alarm went off for a car accident. Kora jumped to her feet, then swore when she was told she wasn't allowed to go. It hurt, but she watched as the trucks and ambulance pulled out. To keep her mind off it, she went to the kitchen to make sure there was a fresh pot of coffee ready for when they returned.

CHAPTER 13

"WHAT THE FUCK!" Seth screamed as he jumped up from the bed and looked around wildly. Kora was on her knees in the middle of the bed with her hands over her ears, and sighed in relief when the loud screeching from what sounded like a bullhorn suddenly stopped. They heard pounding on the stairs, and Kora had just grabbed the covers to cover her naked body when the bedroom door was thrust open, and Trent stood there in the doorway. He caught sight of Seth's naked body and quickly turned his back on them.

"Sorry, so sorry, God, I'm so sorry. I just wanted you to know that it was me. You never set your alarm, and I didn't want you to come down with a loaded gun and shoot me."

"Get out," Seth said as he walked over and

pushed Trent into the hall. "I'll be down in a few. Start the damn coffee." He slammed the door in Trent's face when he tried to look inside the room, Seth could only assume it was to get a look at Kora's naked body. "You probably should put some clothes on!" Trent yelled, then ran away when the door whipped open, and he caught the look on Seth's face. He quickly scrambled away when the door was slammed again. Once the door was firmly closed, and locked for good measure, Seth turned toward the woman in his bed, and chuckled when there was nothing to see but a long lump in the center of the bed. Kora had completely covered herself with the blankets and nothing showed. He walked over to the foot of the bed, and lifted the blanket enough to see her toes, and lightly ran a finger over the bottom of her foot. He broke out into a gigantic grin when she started kicking him, and he dropped down on the bed, wrapped his arms around her legs and proceeded to tickle her feet.

"Stop," she cried out while laughing. "Seth, please stop, or I'm going to pee." Seth looked at her, and immediately released her. She shoved him away from her, kicked herself out from beneath the covers, and ran to the connecting bath. Laughing, Seth followed her, and didn't pay her any attention while he strode into the bathroom, and turned on the shower.

"A little privacy here, Falco." Kora scowled at him, and he looked at her with a quirked brow.

"I've been all over that body with my hands and mouth, and I've been inside you with my cock, fingers, and tongue. I don't think you relieving yourself is going to embarrass me. If it does you, then you should have shut and locked the door behind you." He stood there with his arms crossed over his chest, but turned his back to her to give her a little sense of privacy. When she flushed, she washed her hands and turned to look at him.

"Tell me," she said, and he turned back around to face her. "What was all that noise about?"

Seth walked toward her, and lifted her arm as he bent down in remove the bandage over her stitches, and explained. "Remember I told you that all my brothers have a key to my place?"

"Yes, but that doesn't explain the bullhorn waking us up."

Seth smiled at her. "It's the house alarm, I don't usually set it, but with your attack, I took the precaution of doing so. I just forgot to tell the others I had set it."

"Since when do you have a house alarm? Not that it's any of my business, but you don't seem like the type to have one."

"I wouldn't normally, but after someone got on to the ranch and sabotaged Marcus' helicopter, we've all gone to the length of getting state-of-the-art alarm systems. We even know the codes to the others. I set the alarm as an added protection to keep you safe." He stood to his full height, took her badly bruised face in his hands, and bent down to gently kiss her nose. "I will do anything to help keep you safe. I will fight for you Kora. I will fight anyone or anything that thinks they can get to you." He kissed her mouth when she went to say something, then turned around and opened the shower door. "We best get cleaned up, or the others will be up here wondering where the hell we are."

Kora didn't know what to say to his actions, his tenderness, or his words. She took a couple of extra seconds before joining him in the shower to control her emotions. After drawing in a deep breath, she held it for a few seconds, then let it out slowly before she walked over, opened the shower door, and stepped inside. She didn't know whether she enjoyed it when Seth immediately began to wash her, or if it annoyed her that he was treating her with kid gloves. When they had come home after their shift at the firehouse, he hadn't allowed her to do anything, and God forbid if she winced while lifting her go bag. For now, she would take his coddling, because she had a feeling, he had never done it with anyone before.

"Tip your head back," Seth said, and began massaging shampoo into her long hair. That she could get used to on a daily basis, so she stood there and let him wash her hair. When they were done, he shut the water off, reached out and grabbed a towel to first wrap around his hips, then one around her, handing her another one for her hair.

"Want to have sex?" she hedged to ask, and sighed in frustration when Seth gave her a look.

"It's not that I don't want to, but one, I don't want to pull on your stitches, two, do you really want to take the chance that my brothers won't be standing outside the bedroom door when we open it? Do you really want them to know what we were doing?"

"Fine," Kora sighed and stormed over to her go bag to get out a clean set of clothes. She quickly dressed, and after only tugging the brush through her wet locks, she flounced over to the door, unlocked it, and whipped it open, only to give a small scream. Seth was at her back in under a second to see what had scared her.

"Get out of here!" he yelled at his brothers who stood in the hallway. "What are you doing lurking outside my bedroom?"

"We came to tell you the coffee was done," Troy said, and they all turned when Esme walked up the stairs and glared at the men.

"They're lying, they were in the kitchen taking bets on whether you and Kora were having sex or not."

"Esme!" Troy looked at his girlfriend in feigned shock, then jerked and stumbled forward when Seth reached around Kora and slapped him on the back of the head. Without saying a word, he took Kora's hand in his, and pulled her after him down the hall. At the top of the stairs, he turned back to look at his brothers.

"For that, you guys can both cook breakfast and clean up the mess afterward. I am in the mood for pancakes, home fries, bacon, sausage, and eggs. Along with coffee and juice."

"Why not order the kitchen sink?" Marcus scowled after his retreating back, but Seth stopped and turned back to glare at him.

"Why not eat breakfast at your own place?"

"Fine," the brothers said, and Kora looked back in time to see Esme cover her mouth, but she couldn't stop the giggle that escaped. At the bottom of the stairs, Charli and Tessa stood there with grins on their faces. They only lifted their hands and high-fived Seth as he walked by. Kora shook her head and followed him to the kitchen. She sighed in frustration when Seth grabbed two cups from the cupboard and filled them both, bringing them to the table and holding out the chair for Kora.

"I can get my own coffee, you know."

"I know, but to prove a point, lift your arms above your head."

She did, and when she winced, she saw Seth's mouth tighten, and sighed heavily. "Fine." She sat down and picked up her coffee cup to take her first sip of the day. They were soon joined by the other men.

"Time's wasting boys, and I'm hungry." Seth grinned into his coffee cup as they all glared at him, but invaded his cupboards and refrigerator. In no time pans and griddles were heating up, and food was being prepared. Seth ignored the men and turned to Charli.

"How busy are you these days?"

"She's pretty busy," Marcus said from across the kitchen, and swallowed hard when Seth sent him a look.

"I was talking to Charli," Seth ground out, then scowled at Trent as he pulled a box of baking mix from the cupboard. "Do. Not. Use. That," he said between clenched teeth, and Trent looked at him with a scowl.

"Why not, I always make pancakes with this."

"Use Mom's recipe." His statement caused everyone to pause and stare at him. Marcus was the first to break the silence. "Mom always used that type for our pancakes."

"I'm not talking about Loraine," Seth said, then looked at Heath when he went to take a large breath. "Nor am I talking about your mother. I'm talking about the twins and my mother, Carmen."

After he finished talking, you could hear a pin drop in the entire house, and Kora saw shock on everyone's faces. Before she could say a word, Trent slammed the box of mix on the table, ignoring the fact he had already opened it and some of the powder wafted up and made a fine dust in the air.

"You can *not* be talking about our mother. Hell, she died when Troy and I were three and you were barely seven. The entire house burnt down, and we lost everything. How the hell do you have her recipe for her pancakes?"

"You sure the fuck didn't get it from Dad," Troy said as he stood beside his twin and glared at their older brother.

Seth sighed heavily, then looked his brothers in the eye. "What I'm about to tell you might sound like I have gone off my meds, though I'm not on any, but that's the only explanation I can come up with."

"Spill it," Trent said as he continued to glare at this brother.

"One night after a particularly harrowing mission, I had a dream that I was talking with Mom. It was more like a memory, or so I thought. She was there asking me what would make me feel better. Now in this dream I was a small boy, couldn't have been over three or four, but I immediately told her I wanted her pancakes." Seth turned to look at the women, then directly at Kora.

"Growing up, pancakes were my favorite. I could eat them every day for breakfast."

"Still can," Marcus mumbled, then grinned when the others snorted a laugh.

"Anyway," Seth said as he glared at his youngest sibling. "In the dream I was talking about how good her pancakes were, and how much I loved them. That's all I remember about it. When I woke," he paused as he rose to his feet and walked over to a cabinet closer to the door than the kitchen, where he withdrew a black leather notebook. He pulled it down, and flipped it to the inside cover. "This paper was lying on my nightstand the next morning when I awoke."

The others all crowded around him to stare at the recipe, and it was Kora that frowned as she said, "That is not your handwriting. I've seen it enough on the reports at the station to know that you did not write that."

"I know, it's Mom's handwriting." He looked at the twins and shrugged. "I don't know what else to tell you other than that was some very intense woohoo shit I experienced."

"You try this recipe?" Trent asked as he pulled his phone and snapped a photo of it instead of trying to take the book from him.

"Not yet," Seth closed the book and went back to the table and watched as his brothers hovered over Trent's phone before pulling ingredients out of the cupboards.

"Anyway, Charli, how are you doing in your job?"

"Good, I'm busy, and it's steady, but before long I'll run out of work."

Seth nodded as he sipped his coffee and thought, then he drew in a deep breath and let it out slowly. "How long do you think it would take for you and your people to redo my kitchen?"

"Really?" Charli asked in shock. When she'd been doing his bathroom, he said he didn't want the rest of the house touched until he could come up with a plan. "I thought you didn't want to redo the rest of the house."

Seth only shrugged at her. "Times change," he nodded, then sipped his coffee.

"What do you want done?" Charli asked as she rubbed her hands together and grinned.

Troy looked up from frying the bacon, and asked, "Which wall are you going to knock out?"

"None, I want to keep it like it is. Talk to Kora."

"Me?" Kora asked in shock. "Why me? It's your house, your kitchen."

"You came up with the idea, and I like it. I'm going to go with it. Get with Charli on what we discussed. Charli come to me for the money you need, and go to Kora for the ideas." He continued to sip his coffee then leaned back in his chair and studied his family.

"I'm putting this out there now, Charli, I would like the kitchen done before Thanksgiving. I know you guys come here for breakfast every morning, but I'm going to put it out there that I want our first Thanksgiving as an entire family to be here, in this house." When the others stared at him, he shrugged. "It's been a long time coming." His statement seemed to satisfy everyone, and as he sipped his coffee and watched Kora tell Charli of her plans for the kitchen, a sense of calm and rightness settled in his chest. What he didn't see were the grins of satisfaction from his brothers as they stood at the stove and counter cooking breakfast.

CHAPTER 14

"Don't even think about it," Kora said as she glared at Seth three days later as they stood in his kitchen getting ready to go into work. "I have medical clearance, and besides, I was sidelined for a mild concussion, not the stitches in my side. I'm going to work." She stared for the door, and her look must have told him to back off, because she didn't stop as she stormed out.

Seth looked over at Troy, who was dressed in his white shirt, and black pants, which was what he wore being the chief. "Help me out here, Troy."

"Sorry." Troy held up his hands and shook his head as he backed away from his brother. He had stopped in to ask him something about his place, but had walked in on the argument. "If she has medical clearance, there's nothing I can do. I can't bench her if there isn't anything wrong with her, and besides, we're still short-handed. I know it's not nice to wish for a fire, but what we've been called out to since that wildfire last year has been small potatoes and we've been able to handle it without calling in reinforcements. Seth, Kora's a damn good firefighter. I can see you've gotten close to her, and I'm not saying anything bad about that, but you've been on your own for a long time. Let me give you a little advice."

"What's that?" Seth breathed heavily through his nose, causing the nostrils to flare.

Troy swallowed hard at Seth's look, but drew up to his full height and looked his brother in the eye. "Trust Kora to know when her body can't take it. I know I don't have to tell you that you need to have trust in a relationship to make things work, but trust her in this. We've all known her a week or two, but the other firefighters at the station have worked with her for years. I trust them, they trust her, now you need to do the same." The two brothers stood there in Seth's kitchen staring at each other, then suddenly Seth swore.

"Son of a bitch!" He stormed past Troy, ignoring Charli as she walked up the back steps, and ran out to where Seth and Kora parked their vehicles. He waved his hands in the air as Kora tore out of there in her truck, but Marcus drove by, only slowing down enough to give Seth a thumbs up and tore out after Kora.

"She'll be fine," Trent said as he drove up. "Heath already left, I'll call him to keep an eye out for her truck. She's going to the station and I'm sure they'll sandwich her between them on the way. They won't let anything happen to her."

Seth stood there seething, but finally nodded. "I have to have a word with Charli, then I'll be in. I shouldn't be late."

"Got it," Trent said, and Troy slapped him on the shoulder as he walked by to his own truck.

Back in the kitchen, Seth looked at Charli and nodded. "Kora and I emptied all the cabinets yesterday. Everything is packed in boxes and in the living room. Thank you for doing this."

"Hey, you're paying me to do it, and I had the time to start today. I have Melanie coming in about an hour and we can get these cabinets down and outside to pressure wash them. I'm sure I don't have to tell you that you'll be coming home to a mess, right?"

"Well, since I won't be home for seventy-two hours, I hope it's not too much of a mess." Seth chuckled, then went over and kissed the side of her head. "Thanks again." Then he turned on his heel, and left the woman to tear up his kitchen while he was going to work.

❧

KORA SLOWED DOWN on the road, because the truck in front of her seemed to slow down, and when she tried to go around them, she thought she saw the driver shake their head. She looked in her rearview mirror and swore. Resigned to driving at a snail's pace into the station, she settled to follow Heath, allowing Marcus to follow her. As she drove, she calmed down enough to realize that she might have been a little too hasty in yelling at Seth about returning to work that morning. She knew he was looking out for her, but she would be damned if she would let anyone tell her how and when she would report to work. She knew it was probably bad that she had gotten angry, but after being out of work for months, it was good to be back finally. Again, she would be damned if she let some asshat who had some misguided thought that she had ruined his career to take her out any more than he already had.

Kora was jerked from her stupor when the truck before her braked hard and it took everything, she had not to hit the back of him. Once she had her own truck under control, she stared in shock when an unfamiliar truck came barreling down the side road and if Heath hadn't stopped, it would have plowed right into the driver's door of her truck. Breathing hard, she watched as the man backed up, and she quickly grabbed her phone and was able to get three shots from the camera as they rushed away from the near fatal scene.

Kora screamed when her door was whipped open, and Marcus was there in her face. "Are you okay?"

"I'm fine, what about Heath? That is Heath ahead of us, isn't it?"

"I'm fine," Heath said as he ran back from his truck. "The asshole came out of nowhere and it looked like he wasn't going to stop. I wonder why he left the near-accident scene."

"It was him," Kora said as she held out her hands and the men saw them shaking. They looked around in confusion then they were quickly joined by Troy, Trent, and Seth. Seth waded in, took one look at Kora, and pushed his brothers away. Without saying a work, he unbuckled her seatbelt and gathered her in his arms. He didn't know who was shaking more, him or Kora.

"We saw it from about half a mile back. Did you recognize the truck?" Seth asked, but before Kora could answer, Marcus called out to them.

"I just called it in, Sparrow's on her way." They all nodded, and Seth turned back to Kora.

"What did you say?" he asked when she mumbled something against his chest. It took everything he had in him to lift his hand off the back of her head to allow her to answer.

"It was him," Kora sighed, then elaborated at the blank looks on all their faces. "Trumbull. At least I think it was Trumbull. I know the guy driving that truck that would have hit me was the same man who attacked me in the alley behind my apartment." When they continued to stare at her in shock, she had to wait when the sirens sounded and Sparrow Oakley from the sheriff's department arrived.

"What's going on?"

"Attempted vehicular manslaughter," Heath said.

"Come again?" Sparrow stared at him in shock.

They all turned to Heath as he explained. "I was driving into work and Trent called me to tell me to slow down, because Kora was coming up behind me. Don't ask me why she wasn't with Seth," he looked at Kora, like he was looking over a pair of non-existent glasses. "Anyway, I slowed down until she caught up with me. Marcus was behind her, and Trent came up behind him. As you can see, it's not a straight road, but with the hills we can see anyone who comes up behind us. Anyway, I was looking around and this intersection is more open than others. I was able to look down both ways, and I saw a black pick-up truck come barreling toward us on the left. I instinctively slammed on my brakes to avoid a collision. If I hadn't, the truck would have plowed directly into Kora's door. From what I saw, the driver of the black truck was able to slam on their brakes and back up to get out of here as fast as he could."

Sparrow nodded and took notes, when Marcus and Trent backed up his story, she turned to Kora who was still being held by Seth. "What can you tell me about what happened?"

"I'm going to be honest with you here, Sparrow. I wasn't paying that much attention to the road or my surroundings. Seth and I had a slight disagreement this morning and I stormed away from his place angry. I figured when Heath and Marcus boxed me in, I had better pay attention. I was more focused on our fight than the road. But…" She held up her hand and disengaged herself from Seth long enough to reach behind her and get her phone. She accessed the recent pictures and handed the phone over. "They're not very clear, but it's him."

"Him, who?" Sparrow asked as she took the phone and looked at the photos. She looked up in surprise. "They may not be very good, but you have a perfect shot of the license plate as they were leaving the scene."

"Yeah, he had already turned around by the time I had my phone ready." Kora sighed, rubbed her head, winced as she encountered a bruise from her beating a couple of days before, then looked Sparrow directly in the eye. "I don't know if it was Trumbull exactly, what I do know is that guy driving the truck was the guy I ripped the mask off in the alley. My attacker and that driver are one and the same. I would stake my life on it," Kora said with conviction, and sighed in relief when Seth placed a comforting hand on her shoulder.

"It's Trumbull," Sparrow sighed as she pushed buttons on the phone before she looked up. "I just sent those photos to my phone. Results came back late last night from the DNA you were able to get when you ripped that ski mask off your attacker. You were able to get several hairs with the roots intact, saliva around the mouth, and mucus around the nose of the mask. All three areas were tested. Firefighter's DNA are on file because of what you do for a living, you know, in case something happens, it was an easy match, since he was already in the system."

"She didn't injure him when she said she took out his knee?" Seth scowled at Sparrow, and when she took a step back, then stopped, she held up her hands to ward off his anger.

"That was on my list to do today. I know he didn't go to the Fool's Gold clinic. I'm going to call around and see if anyone fitting Trumbull's description came in with a bum knee in the last couple of days."

"What if?" Seth stared and stood taller when everyone stared at him. "I thought I read in his file that he had injured his knee in the arson fire that was a cover up for Chief Jade's death. What if he still had a knee brace at home and used that if Kora fucked him up? He wouldn't need to go to the hospital. I don't know about the rest of you, but from my experience, any pain can be dealt with if you take the metaphoric handful of over-the-counter pain pills."

"You're right," Sparrow sighed. "Or he could have easily had some pain pills from the initial accident still at home."

"I'd add a list of pharmacies to your to-do list," Kora said. "If he didn't go to the doctor, maybe he had refills on his pain meds and filled them instead, knowing he had the brace at home. I know the cats I feed in the alley attacked him at one point, he might need bandages for those."

"I will, thanks. I'll let you guys get to the station. If I have any questions I'll stop by. How long is this shift?"

"Seventy-two hours," Troy said as he nodded to Sparrow, and everyone broke apart to go to their own vehicles. Seth stayed with Kora as his brothers left and he made sure she was okay enough to drive.

"I'm good, a little shaky," she said as she held out her hand, and he only saw a slight tremble. "I'll meet you at the station."

"We have time, I was going to suggest this before you stormed out this morning, but do you want to swing by and feed the cats?"

"Can we?" Kora's entire face lit with hope, and Seth couldn't resist her expression, nor her, so he leaned in and gently kissed her.

"Yes," he said against her lips as they broke apart. "Let me tell the others we'll break off and go to your apartment. We should be about ten minutes behind them." Kora nodded and settled back behind the wheel of her truck and watched Seth as he walked up to each of his brothers and told them what they would be doing. As he walked by her, he leaned in, kissed her again, then headed to his own truck. In two minutes, they convoyed the rest of the way into town, and Kora broke off to go to her apartment, with Seth close on her heels. She didn't know if she was grateful or not when Trent drove around and tooted the horn when he gave them the thumbs-up sign that it was clear of any unwanted visitors. Kora parked in her usual spot, hopped out, and waited for Seth as he parked beside her. When she said it was okay to park there, he looked around before joining her, then together they went into the building.

"Why the stairs?" Seth asked as he stood outside her apartment door and waited for her to use her key. He looked down then grabbed her hand and pulled her away from the door.

"What the hell?"

"Someone broke in," he said as he pulled his phone, then pointed to the doorknob.

"Son of a bitch," Kora sighed, and stayed back to listen to Seth talk to dispatch about the break-in. He hung up and looked at her. "Call Troy and tell him we'll be a few minutes late." She nodded and did as instructed. They only had ten minutes to wait before they turned and saw Sparrow and two other officers step off the elevator. They only stepped back and pointed to the door, but Kora held out her keys to the other woman and shrugged.

"I don't know whether you'll need these or not, but I do remember locking it the day of my attack, because I was going directly to the station after I fed the cats. That's why I'm here now."

"Okay, stand back," Sparrow said as she pulled her gun, then nodded to the two other officers. Seth and Kora watched as she used her foot and Kora gripped Seth's hand so hard that he winced when the door swung open. They exchanged worried looks and waited as the deputies disappeared into the apartment. Ten minutes later Sparrow came to the door.

"Don't touch anything, but come in and tell me if anything is missing." She stepped back and Kora stopped dead in her tracks when she saw the destruction of her apartment. All the cushions on the living room furniture were cut, the stuffing was all over the living room. With Seth at her back, they continued toward the kitchen. The cupboard doors were open, some ripped off their hinges, and all her food was thrown about, even the food in the refrigerator, or what little was left.

Walking down the hall, toward the bedroom, she paused in the hall and only looked into the bathroom. It seemed like all her shampoo, conditioner, lotions, and body washes were smeared over the walls and floor. She looked at the mirror and stared in horror when she saw the words written on the mirror, *"You're a dead bitch!"*

In the bedroom she saw her clothes strewn about, both what she'd kept in the drawers and the closets. The bed and bedding were in tatters, and so were the clothes. She stared back at Seth in shock. "Why is he after me? I don't even know who the fuck this guy is."

"We'll get to the bottom of it," Sparrow said as she laid her hand over her forearm. "I've called for the forensic team to come in and see if they can recover prints. When you get off work, come to the station for elimination of your own."

"You'll want mine too," Seth said. "I was here to help Kora pack a bag before going to my place."

"Okay, but it'll take time, come in after your shift."

"Thanks, Sparrow." Kora looked around, then asked, "Can I see if he did any damage to the cat food?"

"Would you even trust it if it isn't damaged?" she asked and Kora sighed heavily.

"No, I guess I wouldn't. I'm going to go out and see the cats, then I'll leave to go to the station."

"Okay, again, I'll find you if I need anything from you."

They nodded and Seth, with his jaw clamped tight, escorted her out of the apartment, down to the back alley, and watched as she shook his supporting hand off and began to pace. He let her have her anger, and looked around.

"What the fuck is that?" he asked in shock and pointed. Kora whipped around to see what he was talking about, and followed his finger. She laughed and quickly bent down to one knee to hold out her hand.

"This is the cat I've been feeding." She looked up at him with a grin and stared in shocked surprise when the cat came right up to her and began rubbing itself all over her. It had been months that she had been trying to get him to come to her, now it was like he didn't want to leave her. She was able to pet him, then she stood, and told the cat goodbye. It wasn't good enough for the cat because he followed her and actually jumped into her truck when she opened the door.

"Guess it's going to the station with us," Seth said with a chuckle. "Hey, if he, she, it wants to protect you, who are we to deny it? We'll deal with

Troy once we get there. You go directly to the station, I'll stop by and get some supplies. We really need to clock in, so the others can leave from their shift."

"Thanks Seth," Kora leaned up on her toes and kissed him, then climbed into the front of her truck. She didn't know why she said it, but she turned to the cat, and said, "He's the good guy, you can trust him." She giggled when the cat put its paws on the back of the seat, stood on his hind legs and stared at Seth as they left the apartment building.

CHAPTER 15

KORA WALKED into the fire station and grinned when the enormous cat followed her at her heels. She walked into the kitchen, and saw that the people they relieved had all gone, so only her shift was there. She wasn't surprised when she was immediately surrounded by the Falco brothers.

"Is everything okay?" Troy demanded as he reached for her, then jumped back when he felt something sting his shin. "What the fuck is that?"

"Apparently, it's my protector."

"Why do you call it an it?" Trent asked as he looked down at the cat.

"Because, I can't tell if it's a boy or girl yet."

Heath looked up and grinned, "Honey, if you can't tell he's a boy by the balls hanging off his ass, then I'm sorry my brother has such a small dick you can't decipher the male anatomy."

Kora sputtered her shock at his statement, then threw her head and burst out laughing. "Believe me, he is not lacking in that department. In all the time I've been feeding this guy in the alley behind my apartment, I've never gotten close to him before. This is the first time he's come to me, and now he won't let me out of his sight."

"Is he the one that attacked Trumbull the other day?" Marcus asked as he held out his hand and grinned when the cat looked between him and Kora. The cat didn't move until Kora told him it was okay, that he was the good guy. He did that with everyone around him and they were allowed to pet him before Seth arrived back at the station with several bags. Kora laughed when he began removing cat toys, food, dishes, and even a litter pan with the litter. He looked around and went over to a corner and began setting it up.

"What are you doing?" Troy asked in shock.

"Setting up Bruiser's litter pan."

"Bruiser?" Kora asked him in shock.

"Yep, figured if he could put a hurting on Trumbull, and going by his size, I'm betting he did some pretty good damage to the asshole. We'll keep him here at the station, then we'll take him home with us." He held up his hand when she rushed to hug him. "Only on two conditions."

"Which are?"

"First, when we're off shift, we take him to the

vet to get checked out and get his first round of shots. Second, if he takes off in the middle of the night, we don't chase after him. He's used to being out on his own, we don't need you traipsing through the entire town trying to find him when he doesn't need to be found."

"I agree." Kora did a happy dance and looked down at the cat. "You stay with me, and you'll live like a king, Bruiser." Everyone watched as the cat walked over and gave Kora's ankle a headbutt, then did the same with Seth. They excused themselves and went to change into their uniforms, and returned shortly. After getting their assignments for the day, to keep them busy between calls, Kora tried to keep a watchful eye on Bruiser, but he seemed to be all over the firehouse giving it his own personal inspection. It wasn't until lunchtime that Troy asked what had happened at her apartment.

"I know I shouldn't say this without proof, but I'm saying it was Trumbull. There's no way to tell when it was done, I'm betting it was between the attack in the alley and the attempted run-in this morning," Seth said, and everyone looked at him. He only looked at Kora with a raised brow.

"Yeah, that's what I figured too. Three days ago, when I was attacked, there wasn't anything wrong with my apartment. Then this morning, it's trashed, and he tried to run me off the road. I'll be honest, I wasn't thinking clearly when I got to that intersection, if it hadn't been for Heath slamming on his brakes, I don't know what would have happened."

Seth reached over and took her hand in his, the first time he had shown her any affection while on duty at the firehouse, and Kora looked around at the others quickly. When they didn't comment, she turned back to Seth. "I'm good, maybe we should contact Jake or someone with the Brotherhood."

"I heard," came a voice from behind them, and they all turned to see Jake Cogburn standing there. The first thing he did was walk over to Kora, bend down, take her chin in his hand, and moved her head back and forth. "Are you okay?" he asked as he straightened up, and took the seat offered to him.

"Yeah."

Jake then looked at Seth from beneath lowered brows and scowled at Seth. "This happened on your watch?" Before anyone could say anything, Bruiser walked over to Jake and took a swipe at his legs, and Seth saw his claws had been extended, when Jake only looked down at the cat with one brow raised, they had a staring contest.

"Sorry," Jake said to the cat as he reached down and knocked on the side of his leg where Bruiser had taken a swipe at him, and Seth heard the solid sound. "Fake leg, better luck next time. Glad you're looking out for these two." He smirked, then turned back to Seth and Kora. "Sparrow filled me in on the results from the attack in the alley, I didn't want to bring any unwanted attention to the situation, so I waited until I knew you were on shift again."

"Did she tell you about this morning's attempt to run me off the road?"

"She did, she also told me about your apartment. I'm sorry about that, do you have some place safe to stay?"

"She's staying with me at the ranch," Seth said and laid his arm across the back of her chair. "What can you tell us about Trumbull? Do you have anything new?"

Jake looked around and saw the other Falcos there, along with the other firefighters. He knew them all, and they knew what he did for a living, so he decided to tell them all what he had found out. More people to keep an eye on Kora while she was at work.

"I don't recall whether I told you this or not, but I've been running Trumbull's name. It's not pretty."

"What?" Kora asked, then held her breath.

"Yes, Trumbull was injured in the fire earlier this spring. Yes, he was out on medical leave."

"What were his injuries?" Heath asked.

"Torn ligaments in his left knee. Three weeks after the fire, he was working around the house and apparently hadn't listened to the doctor and he reinjured it, having to have surgery. He was put on extended leave from his firehouse, and a high dose of painkillers. Once he healed from the surgery, he was to report for physical therapy, and talk with the company shrink."

"That's the same thing I had to do," Kora said with a frown.

"Yes, and he went to the therapy, but he never went to the shrink. In the interim of him trying to get better, his wife had an affair with someone, we're still looking into that, and left him. She's trying to get as much out of the divorce as she can, like his pension, or part of it, his disability, the house, spousal support."

"Can't get blood from a rock," Seth said as he picked up his coffee cup and took a healthy sip.

"Yeah, but she's trying," Jake said, and looked at Kora.

"What?" Kora frowned at him, not liking how he was looking at her.

"Out with it, Cogburn," Seth said between clenched teeth when the other man kept looking at Kora sadly. "You obviously have something to say. Say it, so we can get on with what we need to do." He looked around at everyone seated at the table and nodded once. "I'm sure I don't have to tell these fine gentlemen that we need to look out for Kora while we're on a call. To be on the lookout for Trumbull." The others nodded, and Jake finally pulled his phone, accessed something, then turned his phone toward Kora.

"What are you doing with my photo on your phone?" Kora asked in confusion.

"That's not you, that's Marcia Trumbull."

"Holy shit," Kora said as she dropped her fork, grabbed the phone, and studied the photo. "We could be twins."

"Exactly, Hank and I think that's why he's coming at you hard. Not only have you bested him in the academy, you beat him out in your position here at Fool's Gold, then you passed your Lieutenant exam, while he failed his. From what we've been able to dig up, you are his work nemesis, while his wife is his personal one." As he talked, Kora had passed her phone around and everyone agreed that the woman on the phone looked identical to Kora.

"Add to the fact that with Kora looking like his wife, and she stepping out on him, along with trying to take him to the cleaners, he's doubled his efforts to go after Kora."

"That's what we believe," Sparrow said as she walked into the kitchen and made a beeline to the coffee pot. She sighed as she filled a cup, took a sip, and turned to the others. "The crime unit is still at the apartment." She looked at Kora. "Sorry, but I can't do anything about the dust they'll leave behind, but I can give you the card of someone that can go in and clean up afterward." She reached in her pocket to pull out the card and handed it to Kora. As she settled into the chair offered her, she turned down the meal, and sighed heavily again.

"I hope you don't mind, but I asked someone to meet me here to get your and Falco's prints. Since it'll be three days before you two get off shift, we didn't want to put the investigation on hold."

"That's fine," Kora said, and looked up when someone she'd never seen before stood in the doorway, and Sparrow waved him in. Introductions were made, and in under ten minutes, both Seth and Kora had their fingerprints taken, and the man left. They stood at the sink to wash their hands, then joined the others at the table. Kora's appetite was gone, so she pushed her plate away and sat back in her chair. She didn't know whether she was shocked or relieved when Bruiser jumped up on her lap, kneaded his paws on her lower stomach, barely missing the stitches on her side, then settled in for a nap.

"Where did you get him?" Sparrow asked. "Station mascot?"

"No, this is the cat that I've been feeding in the alley. I believe he's also the one that attacked Trumbull when he attacked me."

"Good," Sparrow said, then reached over and pulled several hairs off the ass of the cat. Bruiser lifted his head and glared at the other woman, who held up the hand with the hairs and grinned. "Evidence in case we find animal hairs on Trumbull, or in his vehicle when we apprehend him. If there are any, and they match these, we can arrest him."

"You can't arrest him now?" Heath asked. "We all saw him try to run us off the road this morning."

"Did you actually see his face? Or just the vehicle you described to me at the scene?" She watched the emotions flit across their faces, and nodded when they realized they'd never actually seen the driver. She held up her hand to hold off what she anticipated Seth would say next. "The photo Kora was able to take was fuzzy at best. I believe she said it was Trumbull, but without concrete evidence, there's not much we can do at this time. I hate to say this, but we're in a hurry up and wait situation where we have to wait to see if he will do anything again."

"What if he kills her the next time?" Seth demanded.

"I trust that you'll protect her from that occurring, but if it does happen, then we'll have him." She shrugged and held her hands up, "I'm sorry, but that's all I can say for now. Our hands are tied, because he hasn't done anything to warrant his arrest."

"What about attacking me in the alley?"

"We can only bring him in for questioning. We hit a snag when we went to bring him in."

"Which is?" Troy demanded.

"He's in the wind. No one has seen or heard from him since the night before the attack. Not even his wife. I hadn't realized he was going through a divorce until Jake brought it to my attention two hours ago." Everyone sat around lost in their own thoughts, and then they all jerked and jumped to their feet when the alarm sounded, and they were called out to a car accident. Because she was on duty, Sparrow was the first one to hit the ground running, and called out over her shoulder that she would meet them there.

The truck rolled up onto the scene and Troy immediately began barking out orders to the firemen, and because it was still dry conditions, he had several crew members begin spraying water several yards away from the burning vehicle to prevent the fire on the ground from spreading. With that, he watched the rest of his men put the fire out in what appeared to be a pick-up truck. By the time they were done with it, it was a total loss, and he looked over at Sparrow as she approached him.

"What do you think?" she asked Troy and Seth as he walked up to join them.

"I think someone is trying to hide evidence," Kora said as she joined them. She was removing her gloves as she said this and slapped them on her thigh. "Going out on a limb here, but what if this is

Trumbull's vehicle and he's trying to get rid of evidence."

"What evidence?" Sparrow narrowed her eyes and scowled at the other woman.

"That vehicle is the general description of what we gave you this morning when we were almost run off the road. What if he saw me snap his photo? When I did it, there was no telling if I got anything, I think the only thing of use was the license plate as he was pulling away."

They all turned as one to look at the smoldering truck, and looked at Trent when he joined them. "I'm not telling you what to do, but what if you have this towed into the garage and go over it to look for the vin number, run that to see who it comes back to."

"I will," Sparrow said as she pulled the mic on her shoulder and walked away. They looked over at the truck again, and Troy called them all in.

"I think that's…" he started to say, then he lunged forward at the same time Seth and his other brothers grabbed Kora and shoved her to the ground. Marcus was close enough to Sparrow to do the same, and they waited until the shots stopped before they quickly made their way behind the tanker.

"Son of a fucking bitch!" Sparrow screamed as she pulled her gun and looked around. "Where do you think it came from?" she asked, since she knew they were all former military, they might have had a better bead on the location. When she conferred with them, Heath went with her, making sure they both had bulletproof vests on. The others waited for their return and when they did, Sparrow held up a plastic bag.

"At least he didn't polish his brass," she sighed heavily. "You guys go ahead and head back to the station." When they went to complain, she pointed, and they turned to see three more cars arrive. The car in the lead held the county sheriff, Jim Faulkner. The firemen waited for him to join them, and after giving their statement, he waved them off, turned to Sparrow and demanded she show him where she had marked off the area where she and Heath had found the evidence. By the time they came back to the burnt-out truck, the fire trucks were gone, and the crime unit had arrived. "I'll have the vehicle towed to the county lot and have the team up there go over it. You wanting anything particular for them to check out?"

"Yeah," Sparrow sighed as she rubbed her forehead. "The VIN numbers. See if we can't get them, then find out who it comes back registered to."

"Sounds good," Jim said as he waved at the others and strode back to his car, letting Sparrow finish with her investigation at the scene.

CHAPTER 16

TWO DAYS LATER, armed with a long list, Kora went to Troy's office, knocked on the doorjamb, and waited for him to acknowledge her. He looked up, tossed a pen on the files on his desk, leaned back in his chair, and smiled. "What's up?"

"We need supplies," Kora said firmly, and entered his office to lay the list on the center of his desk. She stepped back and allowed him to read it. She had no idea how he did things like this since taking over for Chief Jade. When he looked at her with a frown, she grinned.

"What did you normally do when Jade was here?"

"He'd give me the key to the chief's truck, and I'd go get the supplies for the entire house. It looks like just the bare minimum has been purchased since I've been out."

"Why you?" Troy frowned at her. "Not that I don't trust you, but why you?"

"Have you had anyone else's cooking?" Kora snorted a laugh when he lifted his nose in disgust.

"I have, and I can honestly say some of it is downright horrid, while others are passable. You, on the other hand, I will eat your cooking any day."

"Thank you for that. Within six months of me arriving here years ago, I made a deal with Chief Jade. If he allowed me to cook all the meals, I would get out of cleaning the bathrooms, showers, and general areas. I never shirked my duties in cleaning the equipment, but if I cooked, I didn't have to clean the station."

"I'm assuming that worked out?"

"It did, but I had to purchase the supplies myself, because we've found if we sent someone else, they never came back with the correct things, or the right amounts."

"How so?" Troy frowned at her. "Not that I'm doubting you, but give me an example."

"Here's an example. One day, I wanted to make spaghetti, I sent someone to the store, I forget who it was now, but I sent them to get spaghetti noodles. He came back with one, one-pound box."

"And?"

"And I was feeding sixteen people."

"Oh, shit, now I understand. Esme and I could

eat a one-pound box ourselves with the leftovers we take to Seth."

"Why would you take the leftovers to Seth?"

Troy looked over both his shoulders, then leaned in and waved her in closer. "Don't tell him I told you this, but he doesn't know how to cook. Oh, he can grill a mean steak, but that's the extent of his cooking skills. Why do you think the rest of us cook breakfast. I don't know for sure, but I think on our days off he only has breakfast, maybe a sandwich or two for dinner. That's about the extent of his cooking. You ever notice that when it's his turn to cook here at the station he orders pizza?"

Kora stared at him in shock, remembering all the times she'd seen him sit at the head of the table at home to watch his brothers like a hawk when they cooked. She thought it was to make sure they didn't make a mess, now she wondered if it was because he was trying to learn what they were doing.

"Wow, I did not know that."

"Don't let him know you know, or that I was the one to tell you, I don't know how he would take it."

"Take what?" Seth asked as he entered the room without knocking or asking permission to enter.

Kora had to give Troy kudos for thinking fast on his feet, maybe that was why he was such a great chief. "Going shopping. Kora said the station needs supplies, and I will not allow her out on her own.

Not that I don't trust her, but with Trumbull still on the loose, and you were told by Jake and Hank to keep an eye on her, you're taking her to the store."

"And the farmers' market," Kora made sure to get that little bit of information in.

"Why the farmers' market?" Seth scowled at her. "The store I can understand, but why the farmers' market again?"

"Because, they have fresh fruits and vegetables. It's getting toward the end of harvest season, and I want to get as fresh as I can. Besides..." She didn't know whether this would be a good bribe or not, she didn't know him well enough yet. "They have fresh apples, and I've been craving some home-made apple pie, I can make it like I did a few days ago." Before she even stopped talking Seth jumped to his feet and waved at the door.

"What are you waiting for, woman, let's go."

"You like apple pie, I take it?"

"Love it."

"We'll need to go to the farmers' market again."

"Done," he said, and grinned at Troy, who wore a gigantic grin of his own. "Keys?" he asked, and held out his hand. Troy pulled them from his pocket and tossed them to him.

"Make sure you have your radios with you, you're still on duty. Do you have your turn-out gear with you?"

"In the truck," they both replied, and Kora only reached over, grabbed the list she'd shown Troy and headed toward the door. She stopped and turned back to Troy.

"In the past, I paid for it all, then turned in the receipt to be reimbursed."

"We can continue doing that if you're good with it."

"I am." She nodded and walked out the door ahead of Seth. They were both in the truck and heading to the regular grocery store in minutes.

"WHAT ABOUT THIS?" Seth asked as he held up a box of pre-made pie dough. They were almost done with their shopping in the store, and were in the last aisle. As much as Kora wanted to linger, she knew she had to be in and out if she wanted to go to the farmers' market. She had slotted two hours to do all the shopping, and so far, they were well ahead of her time allotment. She looked over her shoulder and wrinkled her nose at him.

"I make my pie dough from scratch. You can use that if you want, but I won't be using it."

"Oh, I just thought it might be easier to use, you know, faster."

"Do you cook?" She held her breath as she flat-out asked him that.

"No, why?"

"Because, homemade, though it might take longer, tastes better. It's all in the taste. When we get home from shift, I'll start teaching you."

"We don't know what condition the kitchen will be in." Seth scowled at her.

"Then, I'll teach you when we get back to the station."

He started to say something, but there must have been a look on her face, because he tossed the box of dough back on the shelf, and sighed, "Fine." Then he pushed the cart to the next section.

"I take it that you buy for the entire station, for all the shifts?"

"I do. Some firehouses, the one in Denver did, but some fire stations have food for the different shifts, and it's kept under lock and key. Only people on that shift use it. Though we are a fully manned house, we share. We don't pit one shift against another. That's not fair if we're all called in to work the same fire. No one is any different from anyone else. Sure, you're the Captain, and I'm a Lieutenant, but neither one of us lord it over the others. It's the same with the kitchen. I love to cook, and I take pride that everyone enjoys my cooking. If I can cook something to make the others happy, then it makes me happy."

"Do you ever take requests?"

"I do, but it would have to be something that I can cook in the oven, or the crockpot."

"Why? I've seen you cook things on the stove before."

"Yes, but it's stuff that won't get ruined when I turn the heat off and leave to go out on a call." She pushed her cart and began loading up cartons of eggs, then pointed to the milk section and told him how many gallons they would need, along with the different flavored creamers.

As Seth loaded his own cart, he continued, "Roast beef with all the vegetables. I've been craving it for a while, though I have no clue as to why."

"Ummm, that sounds good."

"I'm hoping the farmers' market will have some fresh vegetables for that, and I can buy them cheaper there."

Kora smiled as they made their way up to the check-out counters, and was surprised that they opened a register just for them. In no time they had everything scanned and the bags loaded into the carts. Though they didn't ask for help, the manager sent one of their stock people out with them to help load the bags in the truck. They were soon on their way to the farmers' market.

Seth looked over at Kora, and reached over to take her hand. "May I ask you a question?"

"Sure, what's up?"

"I know you have to turn the receipt into Troy when we get back, but how would you feel if I used my money and bought some things for the house?" Kora gave him the stink eye, he grinned. "Not the firehouse, our house on the ranch."

"Oh," Kora said, then scowled harder. "Actually, it's your house."

"Until Trumbull is caught and behind bars, it's ours. I know we've only been together for a few days, but I don't want you to leave if and when we find the asshole." He lifted her hand then, and kissed the back of it, ending the discussion for now. They pulled into the farmers' market, and Kora pulled out another list, going over it with Seth before they exited the truck.

At one point, she looked at him and laughed. "Do you even know what some of these vegetables are?"

"No clue," Seth admitted, and she liked that he was honest and didn't try to cover up his lack of knowledge with bravado.

"Okay, then instead of dividing and conquering, we can go together." They exited the truck, and in no time, they were in the thick of things. At one point, she looked at him with a heavy sigh.

"What's wrong?"

"If I wasn't on duty, I'd take longer to look around, but since we have to get back to the station, I'm only hitting the booths that I know carry what I'm looking for."

"You come here often?"

"Every weekend I'm off in the fall. I love the fresh-picked apples from here and not the store. I can also get the pie pumpkins." At his look she grinned. "They're pumpkins grown specially to be cooked for the pumpkin for the pies, and breads, or whatever you make out of pumpkin. If you don't mind, could you buy some of them for our house?"

Seth grinned and felt a lump in his throat when she called his house theirs. With her direction, he ended up purchasing not only a bushel of the pie pumpkins, but one of two different kinds of apples that Kora recommended for baking. Whatever that meant. They were able to drive behind the vendors to pick up their purchases and were soon on their way. One hour and forty-five minutes after leaving the station, they pulled back in, and when Seth saw several of the other firefighters standing around, he called them over to help unload the truck.

Once it was all on the counters in the kitchen, Heath, who hadn't been out with them walked in and said to the room at large, "Kora, it's your turn to clean the bathrooms."

Kora looked at Heath, and felt confident when Troy stepped up beside him and gave her a nod. "Do you want roast beef, vegetables, and home-made biscuits for supper, or a clean bathroom? I won't do both."

"Beef and biscuits," Heath said with a grin and rubbed his stomach.

"From now on," Troy said to everyone standing around. He looked and saw the entire crew was present. "We're going back to the way it was before Kora was injured. She said she'd do all the cooking, and pull her weight in cleaning the equipment, but she will not be doing the general cleaning of the station."

"Yes," one of the firemen from the past fisted his hand in the air and gave a whoop. "I'll clean the bathroom." When the Falcos looked at him, he grinned. "Wait until you taste Kora's cooking, you'll be begging to clean the bathrooms, the bedrooms, and doing the laundry." He rushed away, with several others following him. Kora shook her head and chuckled, then pulled the receipts from her pocket to hand to Troy.

Seth had disappeared, but returned in under ten minutes. It had given Kora enough time to unload all the bags and put the items out on the counter. "Keep out the roast, the vegetables, onions, garlic, the fresh mushrooms..." she stopped when Seth covered her mouth.

"Why don't you take out what you need, and I'll put the rest away."

She kissed his palm, then nodded as she went to

do just that. In no time they had the kitchen set to rights, and the only ingredients were the ones needed to make the pot roast. In no time she had given him instructions on what to do, leaving him to cut up the vegetables to add to it, along with the seasoning. As they prepped, and cooked, she explained everything she was doing, and why. She liked that Seth asked intelligent questions, and knew that before long he would know how to cook. As they progressed, she also got out more pans, turned on another oven, and started mixing the dough for the pies. She left Seth to finish cutting the vegetables and put into the two roasting pans. Once she was satisfied, she had him put both pans into one of the ovens.

"Why such a low temperature on the oven?"

"We can cook it low and slow, and it won't be mush if the alarms sound."

"Oh, I always forget that we might be called out at any minute."

"Exactly."

"I cringe at the house when I see the guys cook. I myself like to clean as I go, so that when I'm done, I don't have as big a mess as if I did all the cleaning at the end." She paused, then frowned at him. "Is that why Charli, Esme, and Tessa stay behind when we leave for work? To clean up after the men?"

"Yes," Troy said as he came in and headed to the fresh pot of coffee that had just stopped perking.

He looked at them and grinned, "It was Esme's idea, and the others went with it."

"I did not know this," Seth said, then studied Troy. "Thank you. Make sure to remind me to tell the girls the same thing when we get home."

"Okay, but I'm sure they know." Troy nodded, lifted his cup, and disappeared.

"What now?" Seth asked as he looked around the clean kitchen. He swore it was cleaner than when they'd started.

"Now, we start on the pies."

"Pies as in plural?" Seth scowled, then cocked his head to the side and looked lost, then he grinned. "Math," he said as he tapped the side of his head. "Four pies?"

"I was thinking more along the lines of eight. That would give us sixty-four pieces, giving two slices for everyone with plenty to spare. If there is any left at the end of our shift, in two days, we can leave it for the others."

"There won't be any left," Seth said with confidence, causing Kora to shake her head and laugh. In no time she had him elbow deep in apple peels while she made the dough. An hour after they started on the pies, they were putting the last one in the oven, and this time, Kora set a timer. "These should only take an hour."

"If the alarm goes off?"

"Depending on how much time we have left, we shut the ovens off and haul ass."

"What do you mean depending on how much time they have left?"

"If they have only a few minutes left, yes, we shut the ovens off, but prop them open a little so they don't burn as they finish cooking."

"Oh," Seth said, then reached into the bowl she'd just picked up and grabbed the stray apples that didn't make it into the pies. He grinned as he took the bowl, and shocked the hell out of Kora when he drew dishwater and washed their dishes. By the time they were done, it was time to cook lunch, and this time, Kora had no problem allowing the men to grill burgers, and bring out the left-over salads from the day before. They continued with their routine, and they were able to sit down to the meal she and Seth had cooked earlier that day with no interruptions. In fact, the only call they'd been on all shift had been the one with the burned-out vehicle.

CHAPTER 17

"Holy hell," Kora called out as Seth paused to allow her third orgasm to rip though her. "Stop, I don't know if I can take any more." She huffed, then groaned when he continued to move, not letting up until he himself cried out when he came. It seemed like a long time before he rolled off her, and Kora didn't care, she loved having his weight on her.

Seth finally rolled off, then lay back down and drew the covers up over them. He smiled when she rolled over and cuddled up to him, with one leg thrown over his groin, and an arm over his stomach. They both were breathing hard, but it was worth it after the hot sex they had just had. After leaving the station that morning, they came back to the ranch and found Charli hard at work on their kitchen. He knew it would take time, and he was prepared for it, what he wasn't prepared for was finding that there was nothing in the room at all, except for bare studs. At his shock, Charli explained that since it was an old house, and when she'd taken down some cabinets, she found a few spots where the wall was spongey, so she ripped the drywall out and found places where the two by fours had rotted through, and other places where there was no insulation at all.

Since Seth hadn't spent a winter in the house yet, and he trusted Charli, he gave her the go ahead to continue as she had been doing. He had jumped in to help, but Charli told him it would be better if he went out to help his brothers. He did that, while Kora stayed behind, and because she had the time, she had stripped decades of paint, grease, and grime off the old cabinets, getting them ready for the new paint. The more she stripped, the more she liked the detail in the wood, but knew she would be painting them. She counted at least six colors on them, and she wanted it all gone before she put the final color on. With her doing the cabinets, it freed up Charli and Melanie to do the framing in the kitchen. By the time they cleaned up for the night, Kora was ready for a hot shower, a hot meal, and a soft bed. She got the shower, and the meal was provided by Tessa, who had come home from work, and quickly put a meal together for her and Heath, and made enough to take over to Seth and

Kora. When Kora said she didn't have to do that, Seth elbowed her aside, took the offered dish, and nodded.

"Thanks, Tessa. I appreciate it. I'll get the dish back to you." Then he turned on his heel and walked toward the dining room they were using to eat in. It also held the microwave and refrigerator, since the stove had been removed, along with all the walls, flooring, and counters.

Tessa laid her hand on Kora's forearm and grinned, "It's okay. We know Seth can't cook, and we can't leave him to starve or fend for himself. If it was up to him, he would be having a pizza delivered every night, but since the ranch is on lockdown because of your stalker, it's easy for us to add a few more ingredients to feed him. One more mouth isn't that big of a deal."

Kora wanted to argue, but she remembered the conversation with Troy a couple of days ago and backed off. "Okay, but when we get our kitchen done, I'm cooking for everyone."

"Lasagna?" Tessa asked hopefully, and Kora could only laugh.

"Deal." She hugged the other woman, then went into the house when Tessa turned to go to the golf cart everyone seemed to have to get to each other's places on the ranch. Kora entered the dining room to see Seth had not only set two places for them to eat, but he had dished up the casserole. She sat down and ate, saving any conversation for later. Now it was after eleven at night and they had sat together either watching TV or reading in the living room, like an old married couple, and they had just had sex before going to sleep.

"Can I tell you something?" Seth asked quietly as he used the hand on the arm he had wrapped around her, and played with her hair. His other arm was behind his head.

"Sure, what's up?" Kora asked sleepily as she looked up at him and frowned at the wistful look on his face. "Are you okay?"

"I am, but I don't know how to say this."

"Just spit it out."

"You won't laugh?"

"No," Kora leaned up on an elbow and studied him. "What is it, Seth?"

Seth drew in a deep breath and let it out in a rush, with his eyes on her, he cleared his throat, then said, "I'm content." Her expression must have conveyed her confusion because he began to talk, and Kora didn't know why, but she settled back down and let him talk. As he did, she ran her hand up his abdomen several times, then settled with playing with the hair in the middle of his chest.

"Growing up, life was great until the fire. After we lost Mom and Grandpa, it was hell living with Shawn. You can ask the twins, but he seemed to blame me for everything that went wrong in his life. Be it a woman broke up with him, no money to pay a bill, a call that went sideways. Hell…" He snorted with no humor. "He even blamed me for the prices going up in the grocery store. Said it was my fault the grocery bill was bigger, because I ate too much. If it wasn't for Loraine, I don't know what I would have done. Probably would have run away from home."

"Who's Loraine, again?" Kora asked, trying not to be jealous.

"Marcus' mom. She did her best, but by the time she came on the scene I was filled with hatred for the old man, and it was hard to get through to me. I'm sorry if this is hard for you to hear, because of your experience with him, but I'm only telling you what I went through. Anyway, what I said was for context. I left when I was seventeen, as I told you a couple of weeks ago, the night I found the old man having dinner with a strange woman while Loraine was home with the boys. At first, I was relieved to be out from under his thumb, then the guilt set in."

"For?" Kora asked, then when he didn't reply, she looked at him and saw the anguish in his expression. She only reached up and laid a hand on his jaw. "Seth, what did you feel guilty for?"

"Leaving the boys," he blurted out. "I felt guilty that I had gotten out from under the old man's thumb, that I wouldn't be ridiculed, belittled, or made to feel worthless every minute of every day. I felt guilty that with me gone, he would go after them, and do the same thing. I felt guilty for feeling free to be away from him. It took a long time to realize that all that shit the old man dumped on my head was because of his own guilt for being with Heath and his mother on the night of the fire. A fire that could have been prevented if he hadn't been such a cheap bastard and bought inferior materials. Anyway, it took a long time for me to realize that when the boys and I would meet up on our leave time, they didn't hold it against me. That took a lot of getting used to."

"Why do you think he was so hard on you?"

"Because the older I became, the more I looked like my mother. Sure, Troy and Trent are twins and my biological brothers, but they took after Dad in looks. I took after my mother. Sometimes when I sit in my chair at the table and watch them cook, I get such an overwhelming sense of pride and love come over me that I don't think I can contain it. It's hard to explain, but I sit there and realize that no matter how many times the old man tried to knock me down, verbally, physically, and mentally, as well as emotionally, he didn't succeed. I have my brothers, and I would do anything for them. Again, when I sit there and watch them every morning," he looked at her with a smirk, "Now that the cat's out of the bag that I can't cook." He paused when she grinned at him.

"Yet, you can't cook *yet*."

"Okay, I'll grant you that. Yet, but when I sit there and watch them, I feel like we should have had that growing up. If the old man had loved us like he said he did, he wouldn't have been a bastard to all of us. I feel content, happy, whole, and that I have a home that I wanted to live in after my first one was burned down. I never did find it until we all moved here to the Paradise Ranch." He became quiet, and Kora didn't know what to say, so she continued to run her hand over his chest, and before long, neither one realized they had fallen asleep.

"FUCK!" Seth and Kora both cried out as their phones went off with the piercing ring of a fire alarm. Kora was the first to grab hers and she answered it while Seth answered his. Neither said a word as they looked at each other, then at the same time they barked out, "On our way!"

"Shit," Kora said as she rushed around and began dressing, as did Seth. "This must be bad if they're calling us in from off-duty."

"Yeah, what did they tell you?"

"Apartment fire, that's all."

"Yeah, me too. Did you get the address?"

"I did," Kora said as she rattled it off, then

hurried out of the bedroom. "Where's your turn-out gear?"

"In my truck? Yours?"

"My truck, want to go together or separately?"

"Together, I don't want to think this, but what if it's something Trumbull has set to get you out on the road in the wee hours of the morning to go after you."

"Shit," Kora said as she waited for him to turn off the house alarm so she could slip outside. As soon as she did, she let him reset the alarm, lock the door, as she made a beeline to her truck and grabbed her turn-out gear. She had just tossed it in the front seat when four trucks came barreling toward them with the lights on high.

"Travel between us!" Troy yelled as he slowed down and waited for Seth to hop into his truck. Heath and Marcus led the way off the ranch, with Seth in the middle and Troy and Trent brought up the rear. On the way to the fire, Kora kicked off her boots and was able to get into her turn-out gear. The closer to town, she told him where to go, and she only said, "Trust me, the way you're going will be blocked." They ignored it when Heath and Marcus went straight and Seth took the turn, followed by the twins. After two more turns, they were able to come up behind the fire, and Seth swore when he saw how engulfed the building was. He slammed on the brakes, and jumped out to grab his gear, his brothers did the same, and Kora headed toward the acting commander to get her instructions.

It took a few seconds to get his attention, but when he turned and saw her, he seemed to sigh in relief.

"You alone?" he yelled at her.

"No, the Falcos are behind me," she cried over the sounds of the fire, and the screams of more alarms as more trucks arrived. The man looked over her head, and nodded. "Garrison and Falco, grab a hose and start in. We've only just begun clearing the floors. I've got men on the first and second, make your way up to the sixth floor and work your way back down to meet the others."

"Roger," Seth said as he rushed over and grabbed a hose, as he came back to Kora, he stopped when he heard the chief on duty swear.

"How the fuck am I going to keep you five apart?" he asked as he saw all five Falco brothers standing there.

"One!" Seth held up his hand, then slapped it on the chest of his brothers as he said their name followed by a number. "Heath, two. Troy, three. Trent, four. Marcus, five. Marcus has ladder experience, he can man that, Heath has wildfire experience."

"Gotcha, Troy, I know you, you can stay out here with me. Grab your radio and get on the other side of the building and keep an eye out over there. This bitch is huge, and I can't be in ten places at once."

"Got it," Troy said, and took off at a jog to the other side. Seth didn't wait for any more instructions as he and Kora ran toward the building. He let Kora lead, he wanted to, but figured his superior height would allow him to look over the top of her, and she wouldn't miss seeing her surroundings. At the entrance they looked at each other as they drew on their masks and made sure their air tanks were secure and on. With a nod to one another, they entered the building and immediately started up the stairs. When they arrived on the sixth floor, Kora turned to Seth with wide eyes. Seth immediately barked into his radio.

"Three, call arson in."

"What?" two people said at the same time.

"We have a pattern here and it smells like it was set. You're going to want to have someone on scene when this bitch is out to come in and investigate." As soon as Seth said that, several more firefighters started saying the same thing. He trusted his brother to get things done, and the proper people notified.

What seemed like hours, but was only about twenty minutes later, both Kora and Seth came out of different rooms and nodded. "Sixth floor clear," Kora said. "Going down to the fifth." They had heard other firefighters calling out that the first, second, and third floors were clear. That left only the fourth and fifth left to clear. Kora was the first down the stairs, aiming their hose to the stairway. The first apartment she kicked the door in was clear after going into all the rooms. She then heard Seth over the radio.

"Two, get on the roof and vent this bitch!"

"Roger," came Heath's reply, and Kora moved onto the next apartment. She had cleared half of it when she burst through a door and yelled.

"Fire department! Call out!" She paused, then repeated it, and thought she heard a cough. She immediately dropped to the floor, then she heard it again, and while still low to the ground, she made her way to the closet.

"Fire department! I've got you." She found two children around the ages of eight to ten, and called it in on her radio.

"I have two with me, bringing them out," she said, and told them what to do, and with her hand on their heads to keep them low, she escorted them out. At the door of the apartment, Seth was there, and he continued to guide them. As soon as he had one child, the stairs in front of them collapsed, and he yelled into his radio.

"Five, get that ladder to the north west window on the west side of the building. We have two victims coming out. The stairway's collapsed, we're all coming out that way! The rest of the floor is clear, get an ambulance there too!"

"Roger!" Marcus said, and Seth turned to start down the hallway, leaving Kora to bring the other victim and follow.

"Four here!" Trent said as he climbed in the window from the ladder and took the child from Seth. Seth immediately turned to go back to Kora. He reached them, grabbed the child, and handed her off to another fireman that had been helping them on the fifth floor. The only way out was through the window.

"Come on!" Seth yelled at Kora as he held his hand out to her to help her though the doorway to the apartment and into the hall so they could both run like hell to the window. He looked over his shoulder and saw the last fireman hand the kid off, and climb out onto the ladder. He looked back and felt Kora's hand in his, just before he tightened his grip, she took a step toward him, and in a blink of an eye, his world fell apart, because the floor beneath Kora's feet was there one step and gone the next. She stared at him with wide eyes as her glove came off in his hand and she plummeted into the abyss of the burning building beneath her.

"KORA!" Seth screamed, and called into the radio. "Three, the floor disappeared beneath Garrison, she fell into the flames. I'm coming down, someone on the bottom go in and find her." He looked up and saw Heath and Trent standing on either side of him, then Marcus was coming through the window. They looked into the hole, and in what felt like hours, but was only seconds, Heath had rigged Seth up with gear to lower him down.

"When you find her, call out what floor," Heath yelled. "We'll come to you." Seth nodded and looked into the flames as he was lowered. He had the forethought to bring the hose with him, and he sprayed as he went, trying to see where he was.

"I see her!" he yelled and everyone heard the alarm that was going off, indicating that they had a man down. It only went off if the person wearing it was prone for a certain length of time. It was so the other firefighters would be able to find them.

"Where are you!" came a voice, and in his haste to get to Kora, Seth didn't recognize the name. "This is Three. One, where are you?"

"Basement, there's no smoke of flames here yet, she fell all the way to the basement. Two, Four, and Five, get your asses down here, best come in the front and make your way down. We're going to need a collar, a backboard, and a ladder."

"Why the ladder?" The first chief asked.

"Because we won't be able to carry her out with the building above us falling on our heads. We'll strap her to the ladder and pull her out of the fucking window."

"This is Five, on it!" Marcus yelled and Seth made his way over to Kora. As much as he wanted to turn off the irritating signal, he needed it to continue to sound, so his brothers could find him. He found Kora lying on her side and he swore when he saw the shield on her face mask had shattered.

"What?" Troy asked. "Talk to me, One, tell me what you see. We need to know what we need on the outside to help her.

"She's on her left side, the shield on her face-mask is shattered. I'm feeling for lumps on her head now." He removed his gloves and ran his hand over her head, and swore. "Three lumps on the side and back of the head. Bloody." He looked up when he saw movement through the smoke across from him as Heath and Trent slid in on her other side. They turned off the alarm and handed Seth the collar. He put it on her and then a backboard arrived, they laid it against her back, rolled her over and strapped her in.

"Helmet?" Trent asked between clenched teeth. They all looked around wildly and it was Heath who found it several feet away. He went for it, laid it on her chest, and together the three of them lifted her and started toward the window Marcus had told them where the ladder was.

"WATCH OUT!" Trent screamed as the rooms above them started falling in on them. They ended up dropping Kora, and the three of them covered her with their own bodies. When it stopped, they looked over as two more pairs of hands joined them, and Seth almost cried in relief when he saw his other two brothers, Marcus and Troy, helping him get Kora out. At the ladder, they strapped the backboard to it and Troy used his radio to signal them to pull it out. As soon as the people on the outside had Kora out, they put the ladder back in the window, and that was how they climbed out of the basement. Just as Troy came out and fell onto the ground, the entire inside of the building fell to the basement, the place they had just been. They quickly jumped to their feet and hurried over to the ambulance and other firefighters, who had been ordered out and they watched it burn.

Seth was over at the ambulance watching as they worked on Kora. When they loaded her in the vehicle, he hopped in and only turned to tell Troy he was going with them. He was waved away and the last thing he saw before they left the scene was Esme as she approached the chief in charge and began talking with him. He breathed easier knowing someone had called the fire investigator in. He would bet his left nut that someone had set that fire. He had no clue who, or why, but it was definitely set. Seth watched as they worked on Kora, without saying a word. He kept gathering the clothes they peeled off her to get to her chest to check her vitals. He had lost all sense of time from the second he put on his mask and entered the building. He happened to glance out the front window and it shocked him that the sun was coming up. They had been called out to the fire at one in the morning, now it was after six. It had felt like only a few minutes, but then when he'd seen Kora fall, it had felt like it had taken days to get to her.

At one point, he leaned in and talked to her. He didn't care who heard him. "Fight, dammit, Kora. You fight to come back to me. Do that for me, and I will fight for you on the outside. I'll find out who did this, and I will make them pay, but you have to fight to come back to me. I love you, and dammit you need to fight for me as hard as I'm going to be fighting for you." He sat back and held on as they pulled into the emergency room entrance at the hospital. No one said a word as he exited the ambulance with tears streaming down his soot-covered face.

"WHAT DO YOU KNOW?" Seth jerked awake from a light snooze and looked up to see not only his brothers, but the entire firehouse off-duty employees standing there. There had to be at least thirty people. All of them were still dressed in their turn-out gear, minus their coats, but they wore their fire pants, and boots. They were all soot-covered and sweat-stained. By the looks of them, they came directly from the fire. It had been Heath that asked the question.

"Not a damn thing," Seth said as he sighed heavily and took the cup of coffee handed to him from the local coffee shop. He liked his coffee strong enough to stand a spoon up in it, but drinking it from a vending machine was just a little too hard for him. He sipped the hot brew and stood, stretching. "They're still working on her. I don't even know how long I've been sitting here."

"Hours," Troy said. "You left the scene a little before six, and it's a thirty-eight-minute ride here. It's now going on ten. We stayed to make sure the fire was out, and waited for the initial walk through from Esme and her people. You were right, along with the others. The fire was set. Esme is still doing her investigation, we'll have to wait for her reports to come in."

"The children that Kora found?" Someone in the crowd asked.

"They were treated for smoke inhalation and are in the children's wing. They're fine, just a few bumps and bruises, and a little smoke in their lungs. Their mother had gone to the store for something, and they remembered hearing to wet towels and put them under the door. That's why they were in the closet."

"Shit," all the firemen said, and looked up when they were joined by Sparrow.

"How is she?" She didn't mix her words when she barked the question. She looked fit to be tied.

"Don't know yet, what do you know?"

"I talked with the apartment manager and the other tenants and it appears that Marcia Trumbull was a tenant of that building. I know this wasn't aimed at Kora like the other attacks have been, but

I talked with the apartment manager, and the other tenants. It appears that Marcia Trumbull was a tenant of that building. If what Esme Jade is saying, there's a possibility it may be arson."

"Fuck," Seth said as he set his coffee cup down, and reached up to pull his hair. He stood like that for a long time, then turned wild eyes onto Sparrow. "Was she hurt? Marcia?"

"No, she was at her boyfriend's house at the time of the fire, she's safe."

"What are you going to do about it?"

"We'll wait until we get the results back from the arson investigation, but…" Sparrow held up her hand to hold off the angry men glaring at her. "He is being arrested as we speak."

"For?"

"For setting his personal property on fire to cover evidence in an attempted crime. The truck fire you guys put out came back as registered to him. Sheriff Faulkner had Marcia and her boyfriend down at the station getting her statement, asking questions on his mentality. When all is said and done, and if the evidence can point in the right direction, we can pin the arson on him, the attempts against Kora on him, and the attempted murder of his wife. Though Kora was injured during the course of her job, we may be able to pin something on him about endangering the lives of others. Tell me, Chief," Sparrow turned to Troy with a question. "If the fire hadn't been set would the floor have given way beneath Kora's feet?"

"Right off the top of my head, no, and it could have happened to any one of my guys. It just so happened that Kora was the one to go into that room. It could have been Seth."

"Okay, that's all I need to know. I'm going to go wait in the corner so I can talk with the doctor when they come out." She didn't have long to wait, because as soon as she finished talking, a woman in a white coat come to the entrance of the waiting room and sighed as she saw all the firemen standing there.

"Kora Garrison?" she called out, and Seth was the first one there, with his brothers on either side of him, and the rest of the firefighters behind.

"How is she?"

"Rough," the doctor sighed, but held up her hand to ward off any questions. "I'll tell you what I know. First, she's not out of the woods yet. She has not, I repeat, she has not regained consciousness yet. That's what's worrying me at the moment. Her other injuries we can deal with, it's the head injury that is a concern. Does anyone know what exactly happened?"

"We were at the apartment fire over in Fool's Gold," Seth began. "We had cleared the sixth floor, and made our way down to the fifth. She took one side of the hall, I took the other. She found the two girls that are in the peds ward now, and we were able to get them to safety. I went back to help Kora out into the hall, simultaneously the stairway collapsed, and as I reached for her hand to pull her into the hallway, the floor beneath her feet disappeared. She fell five, no six stories, because she landed in the basement. It took us several minutes to get to her, and when we did, her helmet was found yards away from her body, her face shield was cracked, and I felt at least three bloody lumps on her head."

"Okay, that explains a lot," the doctor sighed again, and held up her hand when they surged forward. "As I said she's rough, and hasn't woken yet. We've assessed her as much as we can and they're prepping her to take her to ICU. She will be there until she wakes, and because of the extent of her other injuries."

"Which are?" Sparrow asked as she stepped up beside Seth.

"Several broken and cracked ribs." The doctor looked at Seth with a frown. "Did she have an air tank on?"

"She did, and it was still on when I got to her."

"That probably explains the broken ribs then. She also has a broken arm, and a broken shoulder. I saw in her chart she was brought in months ago with a dislocated shoulder from another fire.

Unfortunately, that same shoulder is now broken. It will be months before she can return to duty. If any of you know her well, I'd try to convince her to find a different line of work. Not that she's not good at her job, but I'm saying her shoulder might never heal enough to be able to do the work."

The men around her suddenly grew quiet, and the tallest man before her bit out, "What else?"

"Broken ankle, I'm thinking she got that when she landed, or hit something on the way down. Other than what I already said, that's it. Before you ask, I can allow you to see her, but only two people today. She will be in the ICU until she wakes up."

"Is she in a coma?"

"I wouldn't say a complete coma, but she's unconscious. Until she wakes, we won't know what, if any, brain damage she may have sustained."

They watched at the doctor studied them, then looked at them all. "Two people, then we'll take her to the ICU."

"Go," everyone there said to Seth, and the men behind him gave him a small shove in the direction of the doctor.

"Take Sparrow with you," Troy said ,and nodded. "You're going to want to record her injuries, right?"

She nodded and the two of them went to the back with the doctor. "Did she break open her stitches?" Seth thought to ask, and the doctor stopped in her tracks and stared at him.

"The ones on her side?"

"Yes."

"I wouldn't say she broke them open, but there was bleeding around them when she arrived. What happened?"

"She was attacked at her apartment and the guy had a knife." Sparrow nodded. "He's still at large, and Doc, I know you told everyone they could see her, but I'd like to put a restriction on only allowing this man in to see her."

"Why?"

"Because, the man that attacked her is still at large. He has a vendetta against her, thinking she took his job away from him, it's really messed up. The kicker is that Kora is the spitting image of his wife that is cheating on him and filed for divorce. The wife was a tenant at the apartment fire."

"Christ," the doctor said, then looked at Seth. "What's your name?"

"Seth Falco."

"Okay," the doctor nodded then turned to the nurse sitting at the computer. "Please note that only Seth Falco and the police are allowed to see Ms. Garrison. Here and in the ICU, even when she wakes, only Mr. Falco can see her."

The nurse frowned, but her fingers flew over the keys, and she finally noted. "It's in the chart."

"Thank you." They went behind a curtain, and both Sparrow and the doctor had to catch Seth as he caught his first sight of the woman he loved lying in the bed.

"We tried to clean her up as best we could, but that'll have to wait until we get her to ICU." No one said a word as Seth walked up to the bed, took one of Kora's hands in his, and lifted it to his lips. He kissed it, then leaned down and kissed her forehead.

"Fight, Kora. Fight through that fog keeping you from me. I love you, and we will be together again, but you need to fight to come back to me. I'll fight for you on this end. I love you, fight for your life." He kissed her again, then turned and ignored the tears he saw in the eyes of the other two. "When can I return?"

"Not until we get her settled. I'd say at least three hours."

"Fine, I'll go back and clean up and pack a bag. I suggest you find a place for me to stay." He didn't say another word as he turned back to Kora, kissed her forehead, then her lips one last time before striding out.

"Wow, that was intense."

"Yeah, he's the oldest of the five brothers, and from my understanding he did twenty years in the Marines. He was some Commander or something, and is used to having his orders followed."

"I'm not in the military, and this isn't a military hospital, but his look and tone told me not to fuck with him."

"I wouldn't. I have a feeling he's going to take a leave from the firehouse to be with her," Sparrow leaned in and whispered, "He's her protector from the Brotherhood."

"Ah, shit, it's that bad? The guy who attacked her?"

"It's that bad."

"Okay, I'll work something out for when he returns." The doctor sighed and gave instructions to the people who had just arrived to take Kora to the ICU. Sparrow left and went out to see the only person left was Troy.

"The guys took Seth home. He requested leave time, and I granted it, until Kora's awake, or Trumbull's in your permanent custody."

"Hopefully she'll wake soon," Sparrow said as she patted his arm and left the hospital to go out to her cruiser and head back to her office.

True to his word, Seth was back in exactly three hours, and when he was escorted into Kora's room, he scowled at the overlarge chair in the corner. "It's the best we can do, and the chair does lie out flat, so it's like a single bed." The nurse told him at his scowl. Seth only nodded and said his thanks, then he settled into the chair, re-situated it so he could hold Kora's hand and began to write up the report from the fire. He would have it messengered over once he was done with it. The only time he planned to leave Kora's side was to take a piss, and get something to eat. Other than that, he would be a permanent fixture in the room.

CHAPTER 19

FIVE DAYS LATER, Seth walked into Kora's room from the bathroom and stopped dead in his tracks. Each and every time he entered, his eyes immediately went to her, and this time, he saw her eyes were open. He rushed forward and then slowly approached the bed. With her eyes on him, he took her hand. "Hey, don't try to talk, you have a tube down your throat helping you to breathe." He sighed in relief when she barely nodded her head. "Let me go get someone." Again, she nodded, and he rushed out into the hall, only to stop in his tracks when a doctor was coming in the room. "She's awake," he said, and stepped to the end of the bed to watch the action. In under ten minutes the tube was out, vitals were taken, and the doctor seemed satisfied with the answers to her questions. As she was leaving the room, she told Kora she should be moved to a regular room later that day, or the next at the latest.

"Talk to me," Kora said as soon as it was just her and Seth in the curtained-off area. "What are my injuries, and Seth, if you sugarcoat anything, I'm going to kick your ass when I get out of this bed."

Seth grinned, and unable to resist, he leaned down and kissed her soundly on the mouth, then he placed a hand on either side of her head, leaned in and nodded once. "Total of eight broken or cracked ribs. Severe concussion, that's why you've been out for the last five days. Broken ankle, cuts, bruises, three bloody lumps on your head, and last but not least, the doctor doesn't think you'll return to regular duty."

"Why the fuck not?" She tried to sit up, but winced, then cried out in pain.

"Yeah, that's why. The shoulder you dislocated back in the spring, it's broken now."

"Fuck me," Kora sighed, and that was when Seth realized she only swore like a sailor when she was angry, in pain, or pissed. He was thinking she was all three at the moment. "What the fuck am I going to do if I can't be a firefighter? And don't tell me I could sit behind a fucking desk."

"I won't, and I've been giving it a lot of thought."

"What did you come up with?" They paused when the curtain opened, and Jake Cogburn and Sparrow Oakley stood there.

"What's up?" Seth asked.

"I see the patient is awake, when did this happen?" Sparrow asked.

"Half an hour ago. The doctor talked to her, then I told her all her injuries. We're just starting to discuss option of what else she could do if she can't go back to firefighting. What brings you here?"

"Good news and bad," Jake said.

"Bad first," Kora said, and took Seth's offered hand. Jake smirked when he saw it, then grinned. "Seth is off the case of being your protector."

"Why?" they both asked as one.

Sparrow sighed, then stepped further into the cubby, making it a tight fit, but she closed the curtain behind them, then leaned in. "We arrested Trumbull the day after the fire. Because of the arrest, we were able to hold him. The report came back from Esme and her team, the apartment fire was arson, we have evidence and witness state-ments that Trumbull bragged he was going to go after his wife, with the hope his other problem would be there, and he could take the two of them out at once. When he was in custody, he learned you had been hurt, but his wife had been at her boyfriend's. With warrants, we went through his entire house and found evidence that he planned the attack on you, the ransacking of your apart-ment, the attempt to smash Into your vehicle, it was all written down in explicit detail."

"What happened, why is Seth being off the case the bad news?"

"Because the good news was that while Trumbull was in jail, his wife had him served with the official divorce papers. He left a suicide note and hung himself in the jail cell. No one found him for hours, and by the time they did, it was too late, he was already dead."

"Holy shit, he killed himself? Can I ask what was in the suicide note?"

"In a nutshell, he targeted you, because he still believed you bested him in the job at the Fool's Gold station, you took the Lieutenant's exam the same time he did. You passed, he didn't, he blamed you for that."

"That sounds like a coward's way out," Seth said.

"It was." Jake nodded. "He also blamed his wife for conspiring with Kora to make his life miserable. Again, taking the coward's way out and blaming others for his actions. Bottom line is that after the fire he blew his knee out in, the same one that took Kora out for a few weeks, he never bounced back from it. We believe that being home all the time, his wife couldn't handle it and she had an affair, or was having one when he still worked shifts, he was on the permanent night shift at his house, and she had her nights free."

"I understand," Seth said. "And what? He

couldn't deal with being with his wife twenty-four seven and lost it?"

"Something like that, I know they don't give numbers on your psych eval when you have one to return to work, but the guy we talked to said that if you had to have a score of one to one hundred, with eighty-five or above allowing you to return to work, Trumbull's score would have been around a fifteen."

"Holy shit, he was off his rocker."

"He was, and in the end, he couldn't handle the choices he had made out of life and ended it. I don't usually talk ill of the dead, but this guy was a ticking timebomb and something had to be done. I'm only glad he did it to himself, and didn't take anyone with him." They discussed it for a few more minutes before the two of them left, and Jake told Seth to call him once Kora was home. Seth nodded, then turned to Kora, and smiled when he saw her eyes drooping. He sat there with her hand in his as she slept, and pondered on what Jake would tell him. He came to the conclusion that he would help out if needed, but he would be Kora's permanent protector in the future. Seth had every intention of marrying her when she was ready.

Kora awoke hours later and the first thing she did as soon as she saw Seth was ask, "What were you thinking when you said you know what I can do if I can't be a firefighter? I'll tell you right now, Seth Falco, I will try everything in my power to go back to firefighting, but I would like to know what I could fall back on if it's not possible. Because right now, I have no clue what I would be able to do."

Seth studied her for several minutes, then rose from his chair, sat on the side of the bed, and took her good hand in his. "I know this might be a sexist remark, and if it is, I'm sorry, but what about doing something with your cooking? I have seen all the men at the firehouse, myself included, bend over backwards to help you when you say you want to cook or bake. I'm sure you could open a bakery, or a café, or something." He held his breath and watched her expression, then broke out in a gigantic grin when she pursed her lips, wrinkled her nose, and only nodded.

"It's something to think about," she said. Not denying, or confirming it would be something she wanted to do. He felt by her expression that she would give it a lot of thought before she did anything about it. He knew she would do everything in her power to return to firefighting, but he liked that he was able to give her an option for a different career path if she needed it. She suddenly scowled at him, "This doesn't mean you get out of learning how to cook, now. With me laid up with this damn shoulder, I can tell you how to cook. You won't need to rely on the other women to bring you something."

Seth looked at her in horror, but finally sighed. "I guess I could learn."

"It's a good skill to have," Kora said, tongue in cheek, then brought his hand up and kissed it.

"YOU READY TO BLOW THIS JOINT?" Seth asked as he walked beside Kora's wheelchair as she was being pushed to the front door by a nurse. He carried his bag, and all the flowers that had been sent to her by her friends, and the guys at the station.

"I am." She'd had to stay in the hospital for another five days and was antsy to get home. Now that Trumbull had killed himself, she didn't know whether she was going back to the ranch, or if Seth was taking her back to her apartment. She hoped it was to the Paradise Ranch, with one foot in a cast, with a walking boot over it, and one arm in a sling with a foam with bars to keep her shoulder in place, she was going to need help getting around. Thank goodness for the boot, because she would never be able to use crutches.

"Go get the truck," she said to him, and frowned when he only grinned at her. They approached the entrance and Kora wasn't paying any attention until she was rolled outside and there had to have been at least a hundred firemen and women there who started to applaud when she was rolled out.

Kora stared in shock and looked at Seth. "You did this?"

"Nope," he said as he grinned at her, and pointed. Kora looked over and saw the four Falco brothers break apart from the others and approach with gigantic grins on their faces.

"We planned this," Troy said as he bent over at the waist and kissed her forehead. "We do it for one of our own." The others did and said the same, and Kora tried to keep the tears at bay, but wasn't very successful at it. She was helped from the wheelchair, and before the others swallowed her whole in a group hug, she saw Seth put his items in the wheelchair, then he turned to her and grinned before he dropped to one knee.

"Kora, I know it's only been a few weeks, but I think I fell in love with you the day I met you. I know I assumed the worst at the time, but you proved me wrong at every turn. I love your passion for your job, your heart for everyone around you. I love you whole, and banged up," he said as he reached up and touched a bruise on her cheek that hadn't gone away yet. "Will you make my family complete and marry me?"

"Yes!" Kora said, and instead of throwing herself at him, he took her hand gently in his, because of her sling, and slipped the ring on her finger. "I didn't know this at the time, but Loraine gave this to me, she told me that out of the ashes of the fire the investigators were able to find my mother's ring, which was her mother's, and when the old man gave it to her to put away for one of the twins, she kept it for me, because I was the oldest. The twins agreed with her that I should have it to give to the woman of my dreams. That is you." He took her face gently in his hands, then bent down and kissed her. The whole crowd broke out in applause again, and Kora looked at her work family, and her soon to be married into family, and felt exactly what Seth had said on the night of the fire. She felt whole, content, loved, and like she had a family of her own.

"I heard you," she whispered. "I fought my way back to you. I would fight anything to be by your side."

"I know, I would do the same for you." He kissed her again. With his forehead on hers, her hands still cradling her jaw, he whispered. "I love you."

THE END

Thank you for taking the time to read this. If you enjoyed this book, please give it some love and leave a review at your preferred site.

If you haven't read the other books in the Team Falco Series, check them out!

Brotherhood Protectors Colorado World
Team Falco
Fighting for Esme - Jen Talty
Fighting for Charli - Leanne Tyler
Fighting for Tessa - Stacey Wilk
Fighting for Kora - Deanna L. Rowley
Fighting for Fiona - Kris Norris

You can contact me at:

E-mail: deannalrowley@yahoo.com

Facebook:

https://www.facebook.com/Author-Deanna-L-Rowley-106623544172360

Website:

https://deannarowley.com/

Goodreads:

https://www.goodreads.com/search?q=Deanna+L.+Rowley&qid=1KYE0zxcp5

BookBub:

https://www.bookbub.com/profile/deanna-l-rowley

TikTok: @deannarowley826

Instagram: deannal.rowley

Twitter: @DeannaRowley2

Again, thank you for taking the time to read this.

Please continue reading for other books available for sale and on pre-order.

Claiming Mia

Re-Claiming Mia

Protecting Claire

Challenging Claire

Taming Sue Ellen

Forgiving Heather

Defending Melody

Saving Kate

Susan Stoker's Universe

Saving Veronica

Lorna's Savior

Keeping Tymberly

Protecting Silver

Elle James' Brotherhood Protectors World

Morgan

Ava

Joyce

Astrid

Janice

Alice

June

Not Her Series:

Not Her Dom

Not Her Choice

Not Her Rebound

Not Her Problem #1

Not Her Problem #2

Not Her His Fault

Not Her Doing

Team Falco

Fightng for Kora

Stand-alone:

Double Trouble for Kali

Ruby's Destiny

Molly's Return

ABOUT ELLE JAMES

ELLE JAMES also writing as MYLA JACKSON is a *New York Times* and *USA Today* Bestselling author of books including cowboys, intrigues and paranormal adventures that keep her readers on the edges of their seats. When she's not at her computer, she's traveling, snow skiing, boating, or riding her ATV, dreaming up new stories. Learn more about Elle James at www.ellejames.com

Website | Facebook | Twitter | GoodReads | Newsletter | BookBub | Amazon

Or visit her alter ego Myla Jackson at mylajackson.com
Website | Facebook | Twitter | Newsletter

Follow Me!
www.ellejames.com
ellejamesauthor@gmail.com

www.ingramcontent.com/pod-product-compliance
Lightning Source LLC
Chambersburg PA
CBHW071404150726
48000CB00001B/156